1 3 5 7 9 10 8 6 4 2

Vintage
20 Vauxhall Bridge Road,
London SW1V 2SA

Vintage Classics is part of the Penguin Random House
group of companies whose addresses can be found at
global.penguinrandomhouse.com

Extracts from *A Man in Love* copyright © Forlaget Oktober 2009
English translation copyright © Don Bartlett 2013

Karl Ove Knausgaard has asserted his right to be identified as the author of
this Work in accordance with the Copyright, Designs and Patents Act 1988

First published with the title *Min Kamp Andre Bok* in 2009 by
Forlaget Oktober, Oslo
First published in Great Britain by Harvill Secker in 2013
This short edition published by Vintage in 2017

www.vintage-books.co.uk

A CIP catalogue record for this book is available from the British Library

ISBN 9781784872663

Typeset in 9.5/14.5 pt FreightText Pro
by Jouve (UK), Milton Keynes
Printed and bound by Clays Ltd, St Ives plc

Penguin Random House is committed to a sustainable future for
our business, our readers and our planet. This book is made from
Forest Stewardship Council® certified paper.

Fatherhood

KARL OVE KNAUSGAARD

Translated from the Norwegian by Don Bartlett

VINTAGE MINIS

THE SUMMER HAS BEEN long, and it still isn't over. I finished the first part of the novel on 26 June, and since then, for more than a month, the nursery school has been closed, and we have had Vanja and Heidi at home with all the extra work that involves. I have never understood the point of holidays, have never felt the need for them and have always just wanted to do more work. But if I must, I must. We had planned to spend the first week at the cabin Linda got us to buy last autumn, intended partly as a place to write, partly as a weekend retreat, but after three days we gave up and returned to town. Putting three infants and two adults on a small allotment, surrounded by people on all sides, with nothing else to do but weed the garden and mow the grass, is not necessarily a good idea, especially if the prevailing atmosphere is disharmonious even before you set out. We had several flaming rows there, presumably to the amusement of the neighbours, and the presence of hundreds of meticulously cultivated gardens populated by all these old semi-naked people made me feel claustrophobic and irritable. Children are quick to detect these moods and play on them, particularly Vanja, who reacts almost instantly to shifts in vocal pitch and intensity, and if they are obvious she starts to do what she knows we like least, eventually causing us to lose our tempers if she persists. Already brimming with frustration, it is practically impossible for us to defend ourselves, and then we have the full woes: screaming and shouting and misery. The following week we hired a car and drove up to Tjörn, outside Gothenburg, where Linda's friend Mikaela, who is Vanja's godmother, had invited us to stay in her partner's summer house. We asked if she knew what it was like living with three children, and whether she was really sure she wanted us there, but she said she was sure; she had planned to do some baking with the children and take them swimming and go crabbing so that we could have some time to ourselves. We took her up on the offer. We drove to Tjörn, parked outside the summer house, on the fringes of the beautiful Sørland countryside, and in we piled with all the kids, plus bags and baggage. The intention had been to stay there all week, but three days later we packed all our stuff into the car and headed south again, to Mikaela and Erik's obvious relief.

People who don't have children seldom understand what it involves, no matter how mature and intelligent they might otherwise be, at least that was how it was with me before I had children myself. Mikaela and Erik are careerists: all the time I have known Mikaela she has had nothing but top jobs in the cultural sector, while Erik is the director of some multinational foundation based in Sweden. After Tjörn he had a meeting in Panama, before the two of them were due to leave for a holiday in Provence, that's the way their life is: places I have only ever read about are their stamping grounds. So into that came our family, along with baby wipes and nappies, John crawling all over the place, Heidi and Vanja fighting and screaming, laughing and crying, children who never eat at the table, never do what they are told, at least not when we are visiting other people and really *want* them to behave, because they know what is going on. The more there is at stake for us, the more unruly they become, and even though the summer house was large and spacious it was not large or spacious enough for them to be overlooked. Erik pretended to be unconcerned, he wanted to appear generous and child-friendly, but this was continually contradicted by his body language, his arms pinned to his sides, the way he went round putting things back in their places and that faraway look in his eyes. He was close to the things and the place he had known all his life, but distant from those populating it just now, regarding them more or less in the same way one would regard moles or hedgehogs. I knew how he felt, and I liked him. But I had brought all this along with me, and a real meeting of minds was impossible. He had been educated at Oxford and Cambridge, and had worked for several years as a broker in the City, but on a walk he and Vanja took up a mountainside near the sea one day he let her climb on her own several metres ahead of him while he stood stock-still admiring the view, without taking into account that she was only four and incapable of assessing the risk, so with Heidi in my arms I had to jog up and take over. When we were sitting in a café half an hour later – me with stiff legs after the sudden sprint – and I asked him to give John bits of a bread roll I placed beside him, as I had to keep an eye on Heidi and Vanja while finding them something to eat, he nodded, said he would, but he didn't put down the newspaper he was reading, did not even look up, and failed to notice that John, who was half a metre away from him, was becoming more and more agitated and at length screamed until his face went scarlet with frustration, since the bread he wanted was right in front of him but out of his reach. The situation infuriated Linda, sitting at the other end of the table – I could see it in her eyes – but she bit her tongue, made no comment, waited until we were outside and on our own, then she said we should go home. Now. Accustomed to her moods, I said she should keep her mouth shut and refrain from making decisions like that when she was in such a foul temper. That riled her even more of course, and that was how things stayed until we got into the car next morning to leave.

The blue cloudless sky and the patchwork, windswept yet wonderful countryside, together with the children's happiness and the fact that we were in a car, and not a train compartment or on board a plane, which had been the usual mode of travel for the last few years, lightened the atmosphere, but it was not long before we were at it again because we had to eat, and the restaurant we found and stopped at turned out to belong to a yacht club, but, the waiter informed me, if we just crossed the bridge, walked into town, perhaps 500 metres, there was another restaurant, so twenty minutes later we found ourselves on a high, narrow and very busy bridge, grappling with two buggies, hungry, and with only an industrial area in sight. Linda was furious, her eyes were black, we were always getting into situations like this, she hissed, no one else did, we were useless, now we should be eating, the whole family, we could have been really enjoying ourselves, instead we were out here in a gale-force wind with cars whizzing by, suffocating from exhaust fumes on this bloody bridge. Had I ever seen any other families with three children outside in situations like this? The road we followed ended at a metal gate emblazoned with the logo of a security firm. To reach the town, which looked run-down and cheerless, we had to take a detour through the industrial zone for at least fifteen minutes. I would have left her because she was always moaning, she always wanted something else, never did anything to improve things, just moaned, moaned, moaned, could never face up to difficult situations, and if reality did not live up to her expectations, she blamed me in matters large and small. Well, under normal circumstances we would have gone our separate ways, but as always the practicalities brought us together again: we had one car and two buggies, so you just had to act as if what had been said had not been said after all, push the stained rickety buggies over the bridge and back to the posh yacht club, pack them into the car, strap in the children and drive to the nearest McDonald's, which turned out to be at a petrol station outside Gothenburg city centre, where I sat on a bench eating a sausage while Vanja and Linda ate theirs in the car. John and Heidi were asleep. We scrapped the planned trip to Liseberg Amusement Park, it would only make things worse given the atmosphere between us now; instead, a few hours later, we stopped on impulse at a shoddy so-called 'Fairytale Land', where everything was of the poorest quality, and took the children first to a small 'circus' consisting of a dog jumping through hoops held at knee height, a stout manly-looking lady, probably from somewhere in eastern Europe, who, clad in a bikini, tossed the same hoops in the air and swung them around her hips, tricks which every single girl in my first school mastered, and a fair-haired man of my age with curly-toed shoes, a turban and several spare tyres rolling over his harem trousers, who filled his mouth with petrol and breathed fire four times in the direction of the low ceiling. John and Heidi were staring so hard their eyes were popping out. Vanja had her mind on the lottery stall we had passed, where you could win cuddly toys, and kept pinching me and asking when the performance would finish. Now and then I looked across at Linda. She was sitting with Heidi on her lap and had tears in her eyes. As we came out and started walking down towards the tiny fairground, each pushing a buggy, past a large swimming pool with a long slide, behind whose top towered an enormous troll, perhaps thirty metres high, I asked her why.

'I don't know,' she said. 'But circuses have always moved me.'

'Why?'

'Well, it's so sad, so small and so cheap. And at the same time so beautiful.'

'Even this one?'

'Yes. Didn't you see Heidi and John? They were absolutely hypnotised.'

'But not Vanja,' I said with a smile. Linda returned the smile.

'What?' Vanja said, turning. 'What did you say, dad?'

'I just said that all you were thinking about at the circus was that cuddly toy you saw.'

Vanja smiled in the way she often did when we talked about something she had done. Happy, but also keen, ready for more.

'What did I do?' she asked.

'You pinched my arm,' I answered. 'And said you wanted to go on the lottery.'

'Why?' she asked.

'How should I know?' I said. 'I suppose you wanted that cuddly toy.'

'Shall we do it now then?' she asked.

'Yes,' I said. 'It's down there.'

I pointed down the tarmac path to the fairground amusements we could make out through the trees.

'Can Heidi have one as well?' she asked.

'If she wants,' Linda said.

'She does,' Vanja said, bending down to Heidi, who was in the buggy. 'Do you want one, Heidi?'

'Yes,' Heidi said.

We had to spend ninety kroner on tickets before each of them held a little cloth mouse in their hands. The sun burned down from the sky; the air beneath the trees was still, all sorts of shrill, plinging sounds from the amusements mixed with 80s disco music from the stalls around us. Vanja wanted candyfloss, so ten minutes later we were sitting at a table outside a kiosk with angry persistent wasps buzzing around us in the boiling-hot sun, which ensured that the sugar stuck to everything it came into contact with – the tabletop, the back of the buggy, arms and hands – to the children's loud disgruntlement; this was not what they envisaged when they saw the container with the swirling sugar in the kiosk. My coffee tasted bitter and was almost undrinkable. A small dirty boy pedalled towards us on his tricycle, straight into Heidi's buggy, then looked at us expectantly. He was dark-haired and dark-eyed, possibly Romanian or Albanian or perhaps Greek. After pushing his tricycle into the buggy a few more times, he positioned himself in such a way that we couldn't get out and he stood there with eyes downcast.

'Shall we go?' I asked.

'Heidi wanted a ride,' Linda said. 'Can't we do that first?'

A powerfully built man with protruding ears, also dark-skinned, came and lifted the boy and bike and carried him to the open space in front of the kiosk, patted him on the head a couple of times and went over to the mechanical octopus he was operating. The arms were fitted with small baskets you could sit in, which rose and fell as they slowly rotated. The boy began to cycle across the entrance area where summer-clad visitors were constantly arriving and leaving.

'Of course,' I said, and got up, took Vanja's and Heidi's candyflosses and threw them in the waste bin, and pushed John, who was tossing his head from side to side to catch all the interesting things going on, across the square to the path leading up to 'Cowboy Town'. But Cowboy Town, which was a pile of sand with three newly built sheds labelled, respectively, MINE, SHERIFF and PRISON, the latter two covered with WANTED DEAD OR ALIVE posters, surrounded on one side by birch trees and a ramp where some youngsters were skateboarding and on the other by a horse-riding area, was closed. Inside the fence, just opposite the mine, the eastern European woman sat on a rock, smoking.

'Ride!' Heidi said, looking around.

'We'll have to go to the donkey ride near the entrance,' Linda said.

John threw his bottle of water to the ground. Vanja crawled under the fence and ran over to the mine. When Heidi saw that she scrambled out of her buggy and followed. I spotted a red and white Coke machine at the rear of the sheriff's office, dredged up the contents of my shorts pocket and studied them: two hairslides, one hairpin with a ladybird motif, a lighter, three stones and two small white shells Vanja had found in Tjörn, a twenty-krone note, two five-krone coins and nine krone coins.

'I'll have a smoke in the meantime,' I said. 'I'll be down there.'

I motioned towards a tree trunk at the far end of the area. John raised both arms.

'Go on, then,' Linda said, lifting him up. 'Are you hungry, John?' she asked. 'Oh, it's so hot. Is there no shade anywhere so that I can sit down with him?'

'Up there,' I said, pointing to the restaurant at the top of the hill. It resembled a train, with the counter in the locomotive and the tables in the carriage. Not a soul was to be seen up there. Chairs were propped against the tables.

'That's what I'll do,' Linda said. 'And feed him. Will you keep an eye on the girls?'

I nodded, went to the Coke machine and bought a can, sat down on the tree trunk, lit a cigarette, looked up at the hastily constructed shed where Vanja and Heidi were running in and out of the doorway.

'It's pitch black in here!' Vanja shouted. 'Come and look!'

I raised my hand and waved, which fortunately appeared to satisfy her. She was still clutching the mouse to her chest with one hand.

Where was Heidi's mouse, by the way?

I allowed my gaze to drift up the hill. And there it lay, right outside the sheriff's office, with its head in the sand. At the restaurant Linda dragged a chair to the wall, sat down and began to breastfeed John, who at first kicked out, then lay quite still. The circus lady was making her way up the hill. A horsefly stung me on the calf. I smacked it with such force that it splattered all over my skin. The cigarette tasted terrible in the heat, but I resolutely inhaled the smoke into my lungs, stared up at the tops of the spruce trees, such an intense green where the sun caught them. Another horsefly landed on my calf. I lashed out at it, got up, threw the cigarette to the ground and walked towards the girls with the half-full still cold can of Coke in my hand.

'Daddy, you go round the back while we're inside and see if you can see us through the cracks, OK?' Vanja said, squinting up at me.

'All right, then,' I said, and walked round the shed. Heard them banging around and giggling inside. Bent my head to one of the cracks and peered in. But the difference between the light outside and the darkness inside was too great for me to see anything.

'Daddy, are you outside?' Vanja shouted.

'Yes,' I said.

'Can you see us?'

'No. Have you become invisible?'

'Yes!'

When they came out I pretended I couldn't see them. Focused my eyes on Vanja and called her name.

'I'm *here*,' she said, waving her arms.

'Vanja?' I shouted. 'Where are you? Come out now. It's not funny any more.'

'I'm here! Here!'

'Vanja?'

'Can't you see me, really? Am I really invisible?'

She sounded boundlessly happy although I sensed a touch of unease in her voice. At that moment John started screaming. I looked up. Linda got up clutching him to her breast. It was unlike John to cry like that.

'Oh, there you are!' I said. 'Have you been there the whole time?'

'Ye-es,' she said.

'Can you hear John crying?'

She nodded and looked up.

'We'll have to go then,' I said. 'Come on.'

I reached out for Heidi's hand.

'Don't want to,' she said. 'Don't want to hold hands.'

'OK,' I said. 'Hop into the buggy then.'

'Don't want buggy,' she said.

'Shall I carry you then?'

'Don't want carry.'

I went down and fetched the buggy. When I returned

she had clambered onto the fence. Vanja was sitting on the ground. At the top of the hill Linda had left the restaurant; she was standing in the road now looking down, waving to us with one hand. John was still screaming.

'I don't want to walk,' Vanja said. 'My legs are tired.'

'You've hardly walked a step all day,' I said. 'How can your legs be tired?'

'Haven't got any legs. You'll have to carry me.'

'No, Vanja, that's rubbish. I can't carry you.'

'Yes, you can.'

'Get in the buggy, Heidi,' I said. 'Then we'll go for a ride.'

'Don't want buggy,' she said.

'I haven't got any leeegs!' Vanja said. She screamed the last word.

I felt the fury rising within me. My impulse was to lift them up and carry them, one pinned under each arm. This would not be the first time I had gone off with them kicking and screaming in my arms, oblivious of passers-by, who always stared with such interest when we had our little scenes, as though I was wearing a monkey mask or something.

But this time I managed to regain my composure.

'Could you get into the buggy, Vanja?' I asked.

'If you lift me,' she said.

'No, you'll have to do it yourself.'

'No,' she said. 'I haven't got any legs.'

If I didn't give way we would be standing here until the next day, for though Vanja lacked patience and gave up as soon as she met any resistance, she was infinitely stubborn when it was a question of getting her own way.

'OK,' I said, lifting her up into the buggy. 'You win again.'

'Win what?' she asked.

'Nothing,' I said. 'Come on, Heidi. We're going.'

I lifted her off the fence, and after a couple of half-hearted 'No, don't want's we were on our way up the hill, Heidi on my arm, Vanja in the buggy. As we passed, I picked up Heidi's cloth mouse, brushed off the dirt and popped it into the net shopping bag.

'I don't know what's up with him,' Linda said as we arrived at the top. 'He suddenly started crying. Perhaps he's been stung by a wasp or something. Look . . .'

She pulled up his jumper and showed me a small red mark. He squirmed in her grip, his face red and his hair wet from all the screaming.

'Poor little lad,' she said.

'I've been bitten by a horsefly,' I said. 'Perhaps that's what happened. Put him in the buggy though and we can get going. We can't do anything about it now anyway.'

When he was strapped in, he wriggled about and bored his head down, still screaming.

'Let's get into the car,' I said.

'Yes,' Linda replied. 'But I'll have to change him first. There's a nappy changing room down there.'

I nodded, and we began to walk down. Several hours had passed since we arrived, the sun was lower in the sky and something about the light it cast over the trees reminded me of summer afternoons at home when we either drove to the far side of the island with mum and dad to swim in the sea or walked down to the knoll in the sound beyond the estate. The memories filled my mind for a few seconds, not in the form of specific events, more as atmospheres, smells, sensations. The way the light, which in the middle of the day was whiter and more neutral, became fuller later in the afternoon and began to make the colours darker. Oh, running on the path through the shady forest on a summer day in the 70s! Diving into the salt water and swimming across to Gjerstadholmen on the other side! The sun shining on the sea-smoothed rocks, turning them almost golden. The stiff dry grass growing in the hollows between them. The sense of the depths beneath the surface of the water, so dark as it lay in the shadow beneath the mountainside. The fish gliding by. And then the treetops above us, their slender branches trembling in the sea breeze! The thin bark and the smooth leg-like tree beneath. The green foliage . . .

'There it is,' Linda said, nodding towards a small octagonal wooden construction. 'Will you wait?'

'We'll amble down,' I said.

In the copse inside the fence there were two gnomes carved in wood. That was how the place justified its status as Fairytale Land.

'Look, *tompen*!' Heidi shouted. *Tompen*, or in correct Swedish *tomten*, was a gnome.

She had been fixated on gnomes for quite a time. Well into spring she had pointed to the veranda where the gnome had appeared on Christmas Eve and said '*Tompen*'s coming,' and when she played with one of the presents he had given her she always stated first of all where it had come from. What sort of status he had for her, however, was not easy to say, because when she spotted the gnome outfit in my wardrobe after Christmas she wasn't in the least bit surprised or upset. We hadn't said a word; she just pointed and shouted '*Tompen*' as if that was where he changed his clothes, and when we met the old tramp with the white beard who hung around in the square outside our house she would stand up in the buggy and shout '*Tompen*' at the top of her lungs.

I leaned forward and kissed her chubby cheek.

'No kisses!' she said.

I laughed.

'Can I kiss you then, Vanja?'

'No!' Vanja said.

A meagre though regular stream of people flowed past us, most wearing summery clothes – shorts, T-shirts and sandals – some in jogging pants and trainers, a striking number of them fat, almost none well dressed.

'My daddy in prison!' Heidi shouted with glee.

Vanja turned in the buggy.

'No, daddy's not in prison!' she said.

I laughed again and stopped.

'We'll have to wait for mummy here,' I said.

Your daddy's in prison: that was what kids in the nursery used to say to one another. Heidi had understood it as a great compliment, and often said it when she wanted to boast about me. Last time we were returning from the cabin, according to Linda, she had said it to an elderly lady sitting behind them on the bus. My daddy's in prison. As I hadn't been there, but was standing at the bus stop with John, the comment had been left hanging in the air, unchallenged.

I leaned forward and wiped the sweat off my forehead with my T-shirt sleeve.

'Can I have another ticket, daddy?' Vanja said.

'Nope,' I said. 'You've already won a cuddly toy!'

'Nice daddy, another one?' she said.

I turned and saw Linda walking over. John was sitting upright in the buggy and seemed content under his sun hat.

'Everything OK?' I said.

'Mm. I bathed the sting in cold water. He's tired, though.'

'He'll sleep in the car then,' I said.

'What time do you think it is?'

'Half past three maybe?'

'Home by eight then?'

'Or thereabouts.'

Once again we crossed the tiny fairground, passed the pirate ship, a pathetic wooden façade with gangways behind, where one-legged or one-armed men with headscarves brandished swords, the llama and ostrich enclosures, the small paved area where some kids rode four-wheelers, and finally arrived at the entrance, where there was a kind of obstacle course, a few logs, that is, and some plank walls with netting in between, a stand with a bungee trampoline and a donkey-riding ring, where we stopped. Linda took Heidi, carried her to the queue and put a helmet on her head, while Vanja and I stood watching by the fence with John.

There were four donkeys in the ring at a time, led by parents. The circuit was no more than thirty metres in length, but most of the animals took a long time to complete it because these were donkeys, not ponies, and donkeys stop when the whim takes them. Desperate parents tugged at the reins with all their strength, but the creatures would not budge. In vain they patted them on their flanks; the accursed donkeys were as motionless as ever. One of the children was crying. The woman taking the tickets kept shouting advice to the parents. Pull as hard as you can! Harder! Just pull, they don't mind! Hard! That's the way, that's it!

'Can you see, Vanja?' I said. 'The donkeys are refusing to move!'

She laughed. I was happy because she was happy. At the same time I was a little concerned about how Linda would cope; she wasn't much more patient than Vanja. But when it was her turn, she managed with aplomb. Whenever the donkey stopped she turned round and stood with her back to its flank while making smacking noises with her lips. In her youth she had ridden horses, they had formed a large part of her life, so that must have been how she knew what to do.

Heidi was beaming astride the donkey's back. When the donkey no longer responded to her trick Linda pulled so hard on the bridle it was as if there was no room left for any obstinacy.

'You're such a good rider!' I called to Heidi. Looked down at Vanja. 'Do you want a go?'

Vanja firmly shook her head. Straightened her glasses. She had ridden ponies from the age of eighteen months, and the autumn we moved to Malmö, when she was two and a half, she had started at a riding school. It was in the middle of Folkets Park, a sad down-at-heel riding hall with sawdust on the ground, which was a wonderful experience for her, she absorbed everything and wanted to talk about it when the lesson was over. She sat erect on her straggly pony and was led round and round by Linda, or on those occasions I went with her on my own, by one of the eleven- or twelve-year-old girls who seemed to spend their lives there, while an instructor walked about in the middle telling them what to do. It didn't matter that Vanja wouldn't always understand the instructions; the main thing was the experience of the horses and the environment around them. The stable, the cat that had kittens in the hay, the list of who was going to ride which horse that afternoon, the helmet she chose, the moment the horse was led into the hall, the riding itself, the cinnamon bun and the apple juice she had in the café afterwards. That was the high point of the week. But things changed during the course of the following autumn. They had a new instructor, and Vanja, who looked older than her four years, came face to face with demands she couldn't meet. Even though Linda told the instructor, things didn't get any better and Vanja began to protest when she had to go – she didn't want to go, not at all – and in the end we stopped. Even when she saw Heidi riding the little donkey in the park free of any demands, she didn't want a ride.

Another thing we had signed her up for was a playgroup where the children sometimes sang together, but also did drawings and various other creative activities. The second time she went they were supposed to draw a house, and Vanja had coloured the grass blue. The playgroup leader had gone over to her and said grass wasn't blue but green. Could she do another one? Vanja had torn up her drawing and then shown her annoyance in a way which made the children's parents raise their eyebrows and consider them-selves lucky to have the well-brought-up children they had. Vanja is a great many things, but above all she is sensitive, and the fact that this attitude is already hardening – and it is – causes me concern. Seeing her grow up also changes my view of my own upbringing, not so much because of the quality but the quantity, the sheer amount of time you spend with your children, which is immense. So many hours, so many days, such an infinite number of situations that crop up and are lived through. From my own childhood

I remember only a handful of incidents, all of which I regarded as momentous but which I now understand were a few events among many, which completely expunges their meaning, for how can I know that those particular episodes that lodged themselves in my mind were decisive, and not all the others of which I remember nothing?

When I discuss such topics with Geir, with whom I talk on the telephone for an hour every day, he is wont to quote Sven Stolpe, who has written somewhere about Bergman that he would have been Bergman irrespective of where he had grown up, implying, in other words, that you are who you are whatever your surroundings. What shapes you is the way you are towards your family rather than the family itself. When I was growing up I was taught to look for the explanation of all human qualities, actions and phenomena in the environment in which they originated. Biological or genetic determiners, the givens, that is, barely existed as an option, and when they did they were viewed with suspicion. Such an attitude can at first sight appear humanistic, inasmuch as it is intimately bound up with the notion that all people are equal, but upon closer examination it could just as well be an expression of a mechanistic attitude to man, who, born empty, allows his life to be shaped by his surroundings. For a long time I took a purely theoretical standpoint on the issue, which is actually so fundamental that it can be used as a springboard for any debate – if environment is the operative factor, for example, if man at the outset is both equal and malleable

and the good man can be shaped by engineering his surroundings, hence my parents' generation's belief in the
state, the education system and politics, hence their desire
to reject everything that had been and hence their new
truth, which is not found within man's inner being, in his
detached uniqueness, but on the contrary in areas external
to his intrinsic self, in the universal and collective, perhaps
expressed in its clearest form by Dag Solstad, who has
always been the chronicler of his age, in a text from 1969
containing his famous statement 'We won't give the coffee
pot wings': out with spirituality, out with feeling, in with a
new materialism, but it never struck them that the same
attitude could lie behind the demolition of old parts of
town to make way for roads and car parks, which naturally
the intellectual left opposed, and perhaps it has not been
possible to be aware of this until now, when the link
between the idea of equality and capitalism, the welfare
state and liberalism, Marxist materialism and the con-
sumer society is obvious because the biggest equality
creator of all is money, it levels all differences, and if your
character and your fate are entities that can be shaped,
money is the most natural shaper, and this gives rise to the
fascinating phenomenon whereby crowds of people assert
their individuality and originality by shopping in an iden-
tical way, while those who once ushered all this in with
their affirmation of equality, their emphasis on material
values and belief in change, are now inveighing against
their own handiwork, which they believe the enemy

created, but like all simple reasoning this is not wholly true either: life is not a mathematical quantity, it has no theory, only practice, and though it is tempting to understand a generation's radical rethink of society as being based on its view of the relationship between heredity and environment, this temptation is literary and consists more in the pleasure of speculating, that is of weaving one's thoughts through the most disparate areas of human activity, than in the pleasure of proclaiming the truth. The sky is low in Solstad's books, they show an incredible awareness of the currents in modern times, from the feeling of alienation in the 60s, the celebration of political initiatives at the beginning of the 70s, and then, just as the winds of change were starting to blow, to the distance-taking at the end. These weathervane-like conditions need be neither a strength nor a weakness for a writer, but simply a part of his material, a part of his orientation, and in Solstad's case the most significant feature has always been located elsewhere, namely in his language, which sparkles with its new old-fashioned elegance, and radiates a unique lustre, inimitable and full of elan. This language cannot be learned, this language cannot be bought for money and therein lies its value. It is not the case that we are born equal and that the conditions of life make our lives unequal, it is the opposite, we are born unequal, and the conditions of life make our lives more equal.

When I think of my three children it is not only their distinctive faces that appear before me, but also the quite distinct feeling they radiate. This feeling, which is constant, is what they 'are' for me. And what they 'are' has been present in them ever since the first day I saw them. At that time they could barely do anything, and the little bit they could do, like sucking on a breast, raising their arms as reflex actions, looking at their surroundings, imitating, they could all do that, thus what they 'are' has nothing to do with qualities, has nothing to do with what they can or can't do but is more a kind of light that shines within them.

Their character traits, which slowly began to reveal themselves after only a few weeks, have never changed either, and so different are they inside each of them that it is difficult to imagine the conditions we provide for them, through our behaviour and ways of being, have any decisive significance. John has a mild, friendly temperament, loves his sisters, planes, trains and buses. Heidi is extrovert and talks to everyone she meets; she's obsessed with shoes and clothes, wants to wear only dresses, and is at ease with her little body, such as when she stood naked in front of the swimming pool mirror and said to Linda, Mummy, look what a nice bottom I've got! She hates being reprimanded; if you raise your voice to her she turns away and starts crying. Vanja, on the other hand, gives as good as she gets, has quite a temper, a strong will, is sensitive and gets on easily with people. She has a good memory, knows by heart most of the books we read to her as well as lines in the films we see. She has a sense of humour and is always making us laugh when we are at home, but when she is outside she is easily affected by what goes on around her, and if the situation is too new or unaccustomed she goes into her shell. Shyness made its appearance when she was around seven months, and manifested itself through her shutting her eyes as if asleep whenever a stranger approached; she simply shut her eyes, as if she were asleep. She still does that on rare occasions; if she is sitting in the car and we bump into a parent from the nursery, for example, her eyes suddenly close. At the nursery in Stockholm, which was directly opposite our flat, after a tentative, fumbling start, she attached herself to a boy of her age called Alexander, and together they ran riot on the playground equipment, so much so that the staff said they sometimes had to protect Alexander from her – he couldn't always handle her intensity. But by and large he brightened up when she came, and was sorry when she left, and since then she has always preferred to play with boys; there is something about their physical and unrestrained side she obviously needs, perhaps because it is uncomplicated and easily gives her a feeling of control.

When we moved to Malmö she went to a new nursery, near the Western Harbour, in the newly built part of town where the most affluent lived, and as Heidi was so small I was the one who had to be responsible for settling her in. Every morning we cycled through the town, past the old shipbuilding yards and out towards the sea, Vanja with her little helmet on her head and her arms around me, me with my knees at stomach height on the undersized ladies' bike, light-hearted and happy, for everything in the town was still new to me, and the shifts of light in the morning and afternoon sky had still not been dulled by the debilitating gaze of routine. I thought it would be no more than a transitional phase, Vanja telling me first thing every morning, with an occasional tear, that she didn't want to go to the nursery; she would like it after a while, of course she would. But when we arrived she would not budge from my lap, no matter what the three young women who comprised the staff enticed her with. I thought it would be best to throw her in at the deep end, just walk away and leave her to fend for herself, but neither they nor Linda would hear of such brutality, so I sat there on a chair in a corner of the room with Vanja on my lap, surrounded by children at play, with the sun blazing outside, but the weather became gradually more autumnal as the days passed. In the break, for a snack consisting of apple and pear slices served by the staff in the yard, she would only take part if we sat ten metres away from the others, and when I agreed to that, me with an apologetic smile on my face, it was no surprise to me, for this was my way of relating to other people: how had she, only two and a half years old, managed to pick it up? Of course the staff eventually succeeded in coaxing her away from me, and I was able to cycle back to do some writing while she shed heart-rending tears, and after a month had passed I dropped her off and picked her up as normal. But sometimes in the mornings she still said she didn't want to go, still cried now and then, and when another nursery close to our flat rang to tell us they had a place free we didn't hesitate. It was called Lodjuret and was a parents' cooperative. That meant that all the parents had to put in two weeks' work a year on the staff, as well as filling one of the many administrative or practical posts. How far this nursery was to eat into our lives we had no idea; we talked only of the advantages it would bring: we would get to know Vanja's playmates and, through the duties and meetings, their parents. It was normal, we were told, for the children to go home together, so soon we would have some relief when we needed it. Furthermore, and this was perhaps the weightiest argument, we didn't know anyone in Malmö, not a soul, and this was an easy way to make contacts. And it was true: after a couple of weeks we were invited to one child's birthday party. Vanja was really looking forward to it, not least because she had just got a pair of gold-coloured party shoes she was going to wear, while at the same time not wanting to go, understandably enough, since she still didn't know the others very well. The invitation lay on the shelf in the nursery one Friday afternoon, the party was a week later on the Saturday, and every morning that week Vanja asked if it was Stella's party that day. When we said no, she asked if it was the day after tomorrow; that was about the furthest extent of the future horizon for her. The morning we were at last able to nod and say yes, we were going to Stella's today, she jumped out of bed and headed straight for the cupboard to put on her golden shoes. A couple of times every hour she asked whether it would soon be time to go, and it could have been an unbearable morning of nagging and scenes, but fortunately there were activities to fill it with. Linda took her to a bookshop to buy a present, afterwards they sat at the kitchen table and made a birthday card. We bathed the girls, combed their hair and put on their white stockings and party dresses. Then Vanja's mood suddenly changed – she didn't want to wear stockings or a dress, there was no question of her going to any party, and she threw the golden shoes at the wall – but after patiently sitting through the few minutes the outburst lasted we managed to get her into everything, including even the white knitted shawl she had been given for Heidi's christening, and when at last the girls were sitting in the buggy in front of us they were again filled with expectation. Vanja was serious and quiet, her golden shoes in one hand and the present in the other, but when she turned to say something to us it was with a smile on her lips. Beside her sat Heidi, excited and happy, for although she didn't understand where we were going, the clothes and preparations must have given her an indication that something unusual was in the offing. The apartment where the party was to take place was a few hundred metres up the street where we lived. It was full of the bustle that marks late Saturday afternoons, the last heavily laden shoppers mingling with kids who have come to the town centre to hang around outside Burger King and

McDonald's, and the stream of traffic passing is no longer purely with a purpose in mind, families on their way to and from multi-storey car parks. Now there are more and more of the low shiny black cars with the bass throbbing through the bodywork driven by immigrant men in their twenties. Outside the supermarket there were so many people that we had to stop for a moment, and when the skinny wizened old lady who usually sat there in her wheelchair at this time of day caught sight of Vanja and Heidi she leaned towards them, rang the bell she had hanging from a stick and beamed a smile that was clearly meant to be engaging but to the girls must have been terrifying. But they said nothing, just looked at her. On the other side of the entrance sat a drug addict of my age, with a cap in his outstretched hand. He had a cat inside a cage next to him, and when Vanja saw it she turned to us.

'When we move to the country I want a cat,' she said.

'Cat!' Heidi said, pointing.

I steered the buggy over the kerb onto the road to pass three people walking so damned slowly, probably thought they owned the pavement, walked a few metres as fast as I could and steered back onto the pavement after we had passed them.

'That could be a long way off, you know, Vanja,' I said.

'You can't keep a cat in an apartment,' she said.

'Exactly,' Linda said.

Vanja looked ahead again. She was squeezing the bag containing the present with both hands.

I looked at Linda.

'What was his name again, Stella's father?'

'My mind's gone blank . . .' she said. 'Oh, it was Erik, wasn't it?'

'That's right,' I said. 'What was his job again?'

'I'm not sure,' she said. 'Something to do with design.'

We went past Gottgruvan and both Vanja and Heidi leaned forward to look through the window. Next door was a pawnbroker's. The shop beside that sold a variety of small statues and jewellery, angels and Buddhas, as well as joss sticks, tea, soap and other New Age knick-knacks. Posters hung in the windows giving information about when yoga gurus and well known clairvoyants were coming to town. On the other side of the street was a clothes shop with cheap brands, Ricco Jeans and Clothing, FASHION FOR THE WHOLE FAMILY, beside it was Taboo, a kind of 'erotic' boutique luring passers-by with dildos and dolls in various negligees and corsets in the window by the door, hidden from the street. Next to it was Bergman Bags and Hats, which must have remained unchanged in terms of interior and range from the day it was founded in the 40s, and Radio City, which had just gone bankrupt but where you could still see a window full of illuminated TV screens, surrounded by a wide selection of electrical goods, with prices written on large almost luminous orange and green bits of cardboard. The rule was that the further you advanced up the street, the cheaper and more dubious the shops became. The same applied to the people frequenting the area. Unlike in Stockholm, where we had also lived in the centre, the poverty and misery which existed here were visible in the street. I liked that.

'Here it is,' Linda said, stopping by a door. Outside a bingo hall a little further on three pale-skinned women in their fifties stood smoking. Linda's gaze glided down the list of names beside the intercom; she pressed a number. Two buses thundered past one after the other. Then the door buzzed, and we went into the dark hallway, parked the buggy by the wall and went up the two flights of stairs to the flat, me with Heidi in my arms, Linda holding Vanja's hand. The door was open when we arrived. The inside of the flat was dark too. I felt a certain unease walking straight in, I would have preferred to ring, that would have made our arrival more obvious, because now we were standing in the hall without anyone paying us the slightest attention.

I set Heidi down and took off her jacket. Linda was about to do the same with Vanja, but she protested: her boots were to come off first, then she could put on her golden shoes.

There was a room on either side of the hall. In one, children were playing excitedly; in the other some adults were standing around talking. In the hall, which continued deeper into the flat, I saw Erik standing with his back to us chatting to a mother and father from the nursery.

'Hello!' I said.

He didn't turn. I laid Heidi's jacket on top of a coat on a

chair and met Linda's eye. She was looking for somewhere to hang Vanja's jacket.

'Shall we go in then?' she said.

Heidi wrapped her arms round my leg. I lifted her up and took a few steps forward. Erik turned.

'Hi,' he said.

'Hi,' I replied.

'Hi, Vanja!' he said.

Vanja turned away.

'Aren't you going to give Stella her present?' I asked.

'Stella, Vanja's here!' Erik said.

'You do it,' Vanja said.

Stella got up from the group of children on the floor. She smiled.

'Happy birthday, Stella!' I said. 'Vanja's got a present for you.'

I looked down at Vanja. 'Do you want to give it to her?'

'You do it,' she said in a low voice.

I took the present and passed it to Stella.

'It's from Vanja and Heidi,' I said.

'Thank you,' she said, and tore off the paper. When she saw it was a book she put it on the table next to the other presents and went back to the other children.

'Well?' said Erik. 'Everything OK?'

'Yes, fine,' I said. I could feel my shirt sticking to my chest. Was it noticeable? I wondered.

'What a nice apartment,' Linda said. 'Are there three bedrooms?'

'Yes,' Erik said.

He always looked so wily, always looked as though he had got something on the people he spoke to, it was hard to know where you stood with him; that half-smile of his could equally well have been sarcastic or congenial or tentative. If he'd had a pronounced or strong character, that might well have bothered me, but he was dithery in a weak-minded, irresolute kind of way, so whatever he might be thinking didn't worry me in the slightest. My attention was focused on Vanja. She was standing close to Linda and looking down at the floor.

'The others are in the kitchen,' Erik said. 'There's some wine there, if you fancy a glass.'

Heidi had already entered the room, she was standing in front of a shelf with a wooden snail in her hand. It had wheels and a string you could pull.

I nodded to the two parents down the hall.

'Hi,' they said.

What was his name, now? Johan? Or Jacob? And hers? Was it Mia? Oh hell. Of course. Robin, that was it.

'Hi,' I said.

'You all right?' he said.

'Yes,' I said. 'What about you two?'

'Everything's fine, thank you.'

I smiled at them. They smiled back. Vanja let go of Linda and hesitantly entered the room where the children were playing. For a while she stood observing them. Then it was as if she had decided to take the plunge.

'I've got golden shoes!' she said.

She bent forward and took off one shoe, held it up in the air in case anyone wanted to see. But no one did. When she realised that she put it back on.

'Wouldn't you like to play with the children over there?' I suggested. 'Can you see? They've got a big doll's house.'

She went over, sat down beside them but did nothing, just sat watching.

Linda lifted Heidi and carried her to the kitchen. I followed. Everyone said hello, we returned the greeting, sat down at the long table, I was by the window. They were talking about cheap air tickets, how they started out dirt cheap, slowly became more expensive as you had to pay one surcharge after another, until you were left with a ticket that cost as much as those from more expensive airlines. Then the topic moved to buying CO_2 quotas and after that to the newly introduced chartered train journeys. I could definitely have offered an opinion about that, but I didn't – small talk is one of the infinite number of talents I haven't mastered – so I sat nodding at what was said, as usual, smiling when others smiled, while ardently wishing myself miles away. In front of the worktop was Stella's mother, Frida, making some kind of salad dressing. She was no longer with Erik, and even though they were good at working together where Stella was concerned, you could still occasionally notice the tension and irritation between them at committee meetings in the nursery. She was blonde, had high cheekbones and narrow eyes, a long, slim body, and she knew how to dress, but she was much too pleased with herself, too self-centred for me to find her attractive. I have no problem with uninteresting or uno-riginal people – they may have other, more important attributes, such as warmth, consideration, friendliness, a sense of humour or talents such as being able to make a conversation flow to generate an atmosphere of ease around them, the ability to make a family function – but I feel almost physically ill in the presence of boring people who consider themselves especially interesting and who blow their own trumpets.

She placed the dish of what I thought was a dressing but which turned out to be a 'dip' on a board beside a dish of carrot sticks and one of cucumber sticks. At that moment Vanja came into the room. When she had located us she came over and stood close.

'I want to go home,' she said softly.

'We've only just got here!' I said.

'We're going to stay a bit longer,' Linda said. 'And look, now you're all getting some goodies!' Was she referring to the vegetables on the board?

She had to be.

They were crazy in this country.

'I'll go with you,' I said to Vanja. 'Come on.'

'Will you take Heidi as well?' Linda asked.

I nodded, and with Vanja at my heels I carried her into the room where the children were. Frida followed holding the board. She placed it on a little table in the middle of the floor.

'And look, now you're all getting some goodies!' Was she referring to the vegetables on the board? She had to be. They were crazy in this country

'Here's something to eat,' she said. 'Before the cake arrives.'

The children, three girls and a boy, went on playing with the doll's house. In the other room two boys were running around. Erik was in there, by the stereo system with a CD in his hand.

'I've got a bit of Norwegian jazz here,' he said. 'Are you a jazz fan?'

'We-ell . . .' I said.

'Norway has a great jazz scene,' he said.

'Who's that you have there?' I asked.

He showed me the cover. It was a band I had never heard of.

'Great,' I said.

Vanja was standing behind Heidi trying to lift her. Heidi was protesting.

'She says no, Vanja,' I said. 'Put her down.'

As she carried on I went over to them.

'Don't you want a carrot?' I asked.

'No,' Vanja said.

'But there's a dip,' I said. Went over to the table, took a carrot stick and dunked it in the white, presumably cream-based, dip and put it in my mouth.

'Mm,' I said. 'It's good!'

Why couldn't they have given them sausages, ice cream and pop? Lollipops? Jelly? Chocolate pudding?

What a stupid, bloody idiotic country this was. All the young women drank water in such vast quantities it was coming out of their ears, they thought it was 'beneficial' and 'healthy', but all it did was send the graph of incontinent young people soaring. Children ate wholemeal pasta and wholemeal bread and all sorts of weird coarse-grained rice which their stomachs could not digest properly, but that didn't matter because it was 'beneficial', it was 'healthy', it was 'wholesome'. Oh, they were confusing food with the mind, they thought they could eat their way to being better human beings without understanding that food is one thing and the notions food evokes another. And if you said that, if you said anything of that kind, you were either reactionary or just a Norwegian, in other words ten years behind.

'I don't want any,' Vanja said. 'I'm not hungry.'

'OK, OK,' I said. 'But look here. Have you seen this? It's a train set. Shall we build it?'

She nodded, and we sat down behind the other children. I began to lay railway track in an arc while helping Vanja to fit her pieces. Heidi had moved into the other room, where she walked alongside the bookcase studying everything in it. Whenever the two boys' capers became too boisterous she swivelled round and glared at them.

Erik finally put on a CD and turned up the volume. Piano, bass and a myriad of percussion instruments that a certain type of jazz drummer adores – the kind that bangs stones against each other or uses whatever materials happen to be at hand. For me it sometimes meant nothing, and sometimes I found it ridiculous. I hated it when the audience applauded at jazz concerts.

Erik was nodding to the music, then turned, sent me a wink and went into the kitchen. At that moment the doorbell rang. It was Linus and his son Achilles. Linus had a pinch of *snus* under his top lip, was wearing black trousers, a dark coat and beneath it a white shirt. His fair hair was a touch unkempt, the eyes peering into the flat were honest and naïve.

'Hello!' he said. 'How are you doing?'

'Fine,' I said. 'And you?'

'Yep, jogging along.'

Achilles, who was small with large dark eyes, took off his jacket and shoes while staring at the children behind me. Children are like dogs, they always find their own in crowds. Vanja eyed him as well. He was her favourite, he was the one she had chosen to take over the role of Alexander. But after he had removed his outer clothing he went straight over to the other children, and there was nothing Vanja could do to stop him. Linus slipped into the kitchen, and the glint I thought I detected in his eye could only have been his anticipation of a chance to have a chat.

I got up and looked at Heidi. She was sitting beside the yucca plant under the window, taking earth from the pot and making small piles on the floor. I went over to her, lifted her, scraped what I could back with my hands, and went into the kitchen to find a rag. Vanja followed me. Once there, she climbed onto Linda's lap. In the living room Heidi started to cry. Linda sent me a quizzical look.

'I'll see to her,' I said. 'Just need something to wipe with.'

People were crowded round the worktop, it looked as if a meal was being prepared, and instead of squeezing through, I went to the toilet, unfurled a hefty handful of toilet paper, moistened it under the tap and went back to the living room to clean up. I lifted Heidi, who was still crying, and carried her to the bathroom to wash her hands. She wriggled and squirmed in my grip.

'There, there, sweetheart,' I said. 'Soon be done. Just a bit more, now, OK. There we are!'

As we came out the crying subsided, but she wasn't entirely happy, didn't want to be put down, just wanted to be in my arms. Robin stood in the living room with his arms crossed following the movements of his daughter Theresa, who was only a few months older than Heidi, although she could already speak in long sentences.

'Hi,' he said. 'Writing at the moment, are you?'

'Yes, a bit,' I said.

'Do you write at home?'

'Yes, I've got my own room.'

'Isn't that difficult? I mean, don't you ever feel like watching TV or washing some clothes or something, instead of writing?'

'It's fine. I get less time than if I had an office, but . . .'

'Yes, of course,' he said.

He had quite long blond hair that curled at the nape of his neck, clear blue eyes, a flat nose, broad jawbones. He wasn't strong, nor was he weak. He dressed as if he were in his mid-twenties, even though he was in his late thirties.

What went through his mind I had no idea, I didn't have a clue about what he was thinking, yet there was nothing secretive about him. On the contrary, his face and aura gave the impression of openness. But there was something else nevertheless, I sensed, a shadow of something else. His job was to integrate refugees into the community, he had told me once, and after a few follow-up questions about how many refugees were allowed into the country and so on, I let the matter drop because the opinions and sympathies I had were so far from the norm I assumed he represented that sooner or later they would shine through, whereupon I would come across as the baddie or the idiot, which I saw no reason to encourage.

Vanja, who was sitting on the floor slightly apart from the other children, looked towards us. I put Heidi down, and it was as though Vanja had been waiting for that: she got up at once and came over, took Heidi by the hand and led her to the games shelf, from which she passed her the wooden snail with feelers that whirred when you pulled it along the floor.

'Look, Heidi!' she said, taking it out of her hands and putting it on the floor. 'You pull the string like this. Then it whirrs. See?'

Heidi grabbed the string and pulled. The snail toppled over.

'No, not like that,' Vanja said. 'I'll show you.'

She placed the snail upright and slowly dragged it a few metres.

'I've got a little sister!' she said aloud. Robin had gone to the window, where he stood staring out into the backyard. Stella, who was energetic and presumably extra lively since it was her party, excitedly shouted something which I didn't understand, pointed to one of the two smaller girls, who handed her the doll she was clutching, took out a little buggy, placed the doll in it and began to push it down the hall. Achilles had found his way to Benjamin, a boy eighteen months older than Vanja who usually sat deeply absorbed in something, a drawing or a pile of Lego or a pirate ship with plastic pirates. He was imaginative, independent and well behaved, and was sitting with Achilles now, building the railway track Vanja and I had started. The two smaller girls ran after Stella. Heidi was whimpering. She was probably hungry. I went into the kitchen and sat down beside Linda.

'Will you go and see to them for a bit?' I said. 'I think Heidi's hungry.'

She nodded, patted my shoulder and got up. It took me a few seconds to figure out the subject of the two conversations going on round the table. One was about the car pool, the other about cars, and I inferred that the conversations must have gone off in opposite directions. The darkness outside the windows was dense, the light in the kitchen was frugal, the creases in the Swedish faces around the table were in shadow, and eyes gleamed in the glow from the candles. Erik and Frida and a woman whose name I didn't remember were standing at the worktop with their backs to us, preparing food. The tenderness I felt for Vanja filled me to the brim, but there was nothing I could do. I glanced at the person speaking, gave a faint smile whenever there was a witticism and sipped at the glass of red wine someone had put in front of me.

Directly facing me was the only person who stood out. His face was large, his cheeks were scarred, features coarse, eyes intense. The hands on the table were large. He was wearing a 50s-style shirt and blue jeans rolled up to the calf. His hair was also typical of the 50s, and he sported side burns. But that was not what made him different; it was his personality, you could sense him sitting there, even though he didn't say much.

Once I had been to a party in Stockholm at which a boxer had been present. He was sitting in the kitchen, his physical presence was tangible, and he filled me with a distinct but unpleasant sensation of inferiority. A sensation that I was inferior to him. Strangely enough, the evening was to prove me right. The party was hosted by one of Linda's friends, Cora, her flat was small, so people were standing around chatting everywhere. Music was blaring from a system in the living room. Outside, the streets were white with snow. Linda was heavily pregnant, this was perhaps the last party we would be able to go to before the child was born and changed everything, so even though she was tired, she wanted to try and stay there for a while. I had a drop of wine and chatted to Thomas, who was a photographer and friend of Geir's; he knew Cora through his partner, Marie, who was

a poet and had been one of Cora's instructors at
Biskops-Arnö Folk High School. Linda was sitting on a chair
pulled back from the table because of her stomach, she was
laughing and happy, and I was probably the only person
aware of the slight introversion and faint glow that had
come over her during these last few months. After a while
she got up and went out, I smiled at her and turned my
attention back to Thomas, who was saying something about
the genes of redheads, so prevalent here this evening.

Someone was knocking.

'Cora!' I heard. 'Cora!'

Was it Linda?

I got up and went into the hallway.

The knocking was coming from inside the bathroom.

'Is that you, Linda?' I asked.

'Yes,' she said. 'I think the door lock has jammed. Can
you get Cora? There must be some sort of knack to it.'

I went into the living room and tapped Cora on the
shoulder. She was holding a plate of food in one hand and
a glass of red wine in the other.

'Linda's locked in the bathroom,' I said.

'Oh no!' she said, set the glass and the plate down and
dashed out.

They conferred for a while through the locked door.
Linda tried to follow the instructions she was given, but
nothing helped, the door was and remained jammed. Everyone in the flat was aware of the situation now, the mood
was both amused and excited, a whole flock of people were

in the hall giving advice to Linda while Cora, flummoxed and anxious, kept saying that Linda was heavily pregnant, we had to do something now. In the end the decision was taken to ring for a locksmith. While we waited for him I stood by the door talking to Linda inside, unpleasantly conscious of the fact that everyone could hear what I said and of my own helplessness. Couldn't I just kick the door in and get her out? Simple and effective?

I had never kicked a door in before. I didn't know how solid it was. Imagine if it didn't budge. How stupid would that look?

The locksmith arrived half an hour later. He laid out a canvas bag of tools on the floor and began to fiddle with the lock. He was small, wore glasses and had the beginnings of a bald patch, said nothing to the circle of people around him, tried one tool after another in vain, the damned lock wouldn't budge. In the end, he gave up, told Cora it was no good, he couldn't get the door open.

'What shall we do then?' Cora asked. 'She's due soon!'

He shrugged.

'You'll have to kick it in,' he said, starting to pack his tools.

Who was going to kick it in?

It had to be me. I was Linda's husband. It was my responsibility.

My heart was pounding.

Should I do it? Take a step back in full view of everyone and kick it with all my might?

What if the door didn't give? What if it swung open and hit Linda?

She would have to take shelter in the corner.

Calmly, I breathed in and out several times. But it didn't help, I was still shaking inside. Attracting attention like this was anathema to me. If there was a risk of failure it was even worse.

Cora looked around.

'We have to kick the door in,' she said. 'Who can do that?'

The locksmith disappeared through the door. If it was going to be me, now was the time to step forward.

But I couldn't bring myself to do it.

'Micke,' Cora said. 'He's a boxer.'

She swivelled to fetch him from the living room.

'I can ask him,' I said. In that way I wouldn't be hiding my humiliation at any rate, I would tell him straight out that I, as Linda's husband, didn't dare to kick in the door, I was asking you, as a boxer and a giant, to do it for me.

He was standing by the window with a beer in his hand chatting to two girls.

'Hello, Micke,' I said.

He looked at me.

'She's still locked in the bathroom. The locksmith couldn't open the door. Could you kick it in, do you think?'

'Of course,' he said, eyeing me for a moment before putting down his beer and going into the hallway. I followed. People moved to the side as he made his way to the door.

'Are you in there?' he asked.

'Yes,' said Linda.

'Stand as far back from the door as you can. I'm going to kick it in.'

'Right,' Linda said.

He waited for a moment. Then he raised his foot and kicked the door with such force that the lock was knocked inwards. Splinters flew.

When Linda came out, some people clapped.

'Poor you,' Cora said. 'I'm so sorry. Subjecting you to that, and then . . .'

Micke turned and went.

'How are you?' I asked.

'Fine,' Linda said. 'But I think maybe we should go home soon.'

'Of course,' I said.

In the living room the music was turned down as two women in their early thirties were about to read their gushing poems. I passed Linda her jacket, put on mine, said goodbye to Cora and Thomas, my shame seared inside me, but the last duty remained, I had to thank Micke for what he had done. I made my way through the poetry audience and stopped by the window in front of him.

'Thank you very much,' I said. 'You rescued her.'

He blew out his cheeks and shrugged his shoulders. 'It was nothing.'

In the taxi on the way home I hardly looked at Linda. I hadn't risen to the task. I had been so cowardly as to let someone else do the job, and all of that was visible in my eyes. I was a miserable wretch.

When we were in bed she asked what was wrong with me. I said I was ashamed that I hadn't kicked in the door. She looked at me in astonishment. The thought had not even occurred to her. Why should I have done it? I wasn't the type, was I.

The man sitting on the opposite side of the table radiated some of the same vibes the boxer in Stockholm had. It didn't have anything to do with the size of his body or muscle mass, for even though several of the men here had well-trained powerful upper bodies they still made a lightweight impression, their presence in the room was fleeting and insignificant like a casual thought. No, there was something else, and whenever I met it I came off worse, I saw myself as the weak trammelled man I was, who lived his life in the world of words. I sat musing on this while taking occasional peeps at him and listening to the ongoing conversation with half an ear. Now it had turned to various teaching styles, and which schools each of them was considering for their children. After a short intermezzo in which Linus talked about a sports day he had attended, the conversation moved to house prices. There was agreement that house prices had soared over recent years, but more in Stockholm than here, and that presumably it was just a question of time before the tide would turn, maybe they would even fall as steeply as they had risen. Then Linus turned to face me.

'What are house prices like in Norway, then?' he asked.

'About the same as here,' I said. 'Oslo's as expensive as Stockholm. It's a bit cheaper in the provinces.'

He kept his eyes fixed on me for a while, in case I might exploit the opening he had given me, but when this proved not to be the case, he turned back and continued chatting. He had done the very same thing at the first general meeting we had attended, though at that time with a kind of critical undertone, because, as he had put it, the meeting was drawing to a close and Linda and I still hadn't said anything, the point was that everyone should have their say, that was the whole idea of a parents' cooperative. I had no idea what to think about the matter under discussion, and it was Linda who, with a faint blush, weighed up the pros and cons on behalf of the family, with the whole assembly staring at her. First on the agenda was whether the nursery should get rid of the cook who was employed there, and instead go for a catering firm, which would be cheaper, and second, if they did that, what kind of food they should opt for: vegetarian or the standard? Lodjuret was actually a vegetarian nursery, that was the principle on which it had been founded in its day, but now only four of the parents were vegetarians, and since the children didn't eat much of the numerous varieties of vegetables that were served up, many parents thought they might as well dispense with the principle. The discussion lasted for several hours and scoured the subject like a trawl net on the seabed. The meat percentage in various types of sausage was brought up; it was one thing that the sausages bought in shops had the meat percentage printed on the label, but quite another what catering companies did with their sausages, because how could you know how much meat they contained? To me sausages were sausages. I didn't have the slightest idea about the world that was opening before my eyes that evening, least of all that there were people who could delve so deeply into it. Wasn't it nice for the children to have a cook who made food for them in their kitchen? I thought but didn't say, and I was beginning to hope that the whole discussion would pass without our having to say anything, before, that is, Linus fixed his astute and naïve eyes on us.

From the living room came the sound of Heidi crying. Again I thought of Vanja. Usually she solved situations like these by doing exactly the same as the others. If they pulled out a chair, she pulled out a chair, if they sat down, she sat down, if they laughed, she laughed, even if she didn't understand what they were laughing at. If they ran around calling a name, she ran around calling a name. That was her method. But Stella had seen through it. Once I happened to be there and heard her say, You just copy us! You're a parrot! A parrot! That hadn't deterred her from continuing, so far the method had proved too successful for that, but now when Stella herself was holding court it probably did inhibit her. I knew she understood what this was all about. Several times she had said the same to Heidi, that she copied her, she was a parrot.

Stella was eighteen months older than Vanja, who admired her above all else. When she was allowed to tag along, it was at Stella's grace, and she had this hold on all the children in the nursery. She was a beautiful child, she had blonde hair and big eyes, was always nicely, sensibly dressed, and the streak of cruelty she possessed was no worse and no better than that displayed by other children at the top of the hierarchy. That was not why I had problems with her. The problems for me were that she was so aware of the impression she made on adults, and the way in which she exploited this charming innocence. During my compulsory duties at the nursery I had never fallen for it. No matter how sparkling the eyes she clapped on me when she asked for something, my reaction remained one of indifference, which of course confused her, and she redoubled her endeavours to charm me. Once she had stayed with us after nursery to go to the park and sat beside Vanja in the double buggy while I carried Heidi on one arm and pushed them with the other. She jumped out a few hundred metres before the park to run the last stretch, which I reacted sharply to. I called her back and said that she was to sit nicely in the buggy until we arrived, there were cars around, couldn't she see them? She looked at me in surprise, she wasn't used to that tone, and even though I was not satisfied with the way I had resolved the situation, I also thought that a *No!* was not the worst thing that could befall this creature. But she had taken note of it, because when, half an hour later, I swung them round by their feet to their immense glee, and then knelt down to fight with them, which Vanja loved, especially when she took a run-up and knocked me over onto the grass, Stella, when it was her turn, kicked me on the calf instead, and that was all right once, all right twice, but when she did it a third time I told her, That hurts, that does, just stop it now, Stella, which of course she ignored, now it had become exciting, and she kicked me again, with a loud laugh, and Vanja, who always aped her, also laughed, whereupon I got up, grabbed Stella around the waist and stood her up. 'Listen to me, you little brat,' I felt like saying, and would have done had her mother not been coming to collect her in half an hour. 'Listen, Stella,' I said instead, harshly, with annoyance, looking her in the eye. 'When I say no, I mean no. Do you understand?' She looked down, refusing to answer. I raised her chin. 'Do you understand?' I asked again. She nodded, and I let her go. 'I'm going to sit on that bench over there. You can play on your own until your mother comes.' Vanja sent me a bemused look. But then she laughed and tugged at Stella. For her, scenes like this were everyday occurrences. Fortunately, Stella dropped the matter at once, for I was really skating on thin ice – what on earth would I do if she began to cry or scream? But she went with Vanja over to the big 'train' which was teeming with kids. When her mother came she had two paper cups of latte in her hand. Usually I would have gone as soon as she arrived, but when she passed me a cup of coffee I had no option but to sit down and listen to her chatter on about her job, while squinting into the low November sun and keeping half an eye on the children.

The week when I'd had nursery duty and in principle had been like any employee ran more or less like clockwork; I had worked a lot in institutions before and soon had all the routines off pat, which the staff were not accustomed to seeing with parents, nor was I a stranger to dressing and undressing children, changing their nappies and even playing if it was required. The children reacted to my presence in different ways, of course. For example, one of them who hung around without any friends, a gangling white-haired boy, wanted to crawl up onto my lap all the time, either to have a story read or just to sit there. I played with another one for half an hour after the others had gone, his mother was late, but he forgot all about that when we played pirate ships. To his great delight, I kept adding new features like sharks and marauding boats and fires. A third boy, on the other hand, the oldest there, immediately discovered one of my weak spots by taking a bunch of keys from my pocket while we were at the table eating. The mere fact that I didn't stop him, even though I was angry, allowed him to follow the scent. First of all, he asked if there was a car key. When I shook my head he asked me why not. I haven't got a car, I said. Why not? he asked. I haven't got a licence, I said. Can't you drive a car? he said. Aren't you an adult, then? he asked. All adults can drive cars, can't they? Then he jingled the keys under my nose. I let him do it, thinking he would soon tire of it, but he didn't; on the contrary he persisted. I've got your keys, he said. And you can't get them. He kept jingling them under my nose. The other children watched us, the three members of staff as well. I made the mistake of lunging for the keys. He managed to pull them away in time, and laughed and jeered. Ha, ha, you didn't get them! he crowed. Again I tried not to show my annoyance. He started banging the keys on the table. Don't do that, I said. He just smiled cheekily and persisted. One of the nursery staff told him to stop. And he did. But continued to dangle them from his hand. You'll never get them, he said. Then Vanja broke in.

'Give the keys to daddy!' she said.

What kind of situation was this?

I acted as if nothing was happening, leaned over the food again and went on eating. But the little devil continued to tease me. Jingle, jingle. I decided to let him keep them until we had finished eating. Drank some water, feeling my face strangely flushed over such a tiny matter. Was that what Olaf, the head of the nursery, saw? At any rate, he ordered Jocke to hand back the keys. And Jocke did, without any fuss.

All my adult life I have kept a distance from other people, it has been my way of coping because I come so incredibly close to others in my thoughts and feelings they only have to look away dismissively for a storm to break inside me. That closeness naturally informs my relationship with children too, that is what allows me to sit down and play with them, but as they lack any veneer of courtesy and decency that adults have, this also means they can freely penetrate the outer bulwarks of my personality and then wreak as much havoc as they wish. My only defence, when it all started, was either sheer physical strength, which I was not able to use, or else simply to pretend I wasn't bothered, possibly the best approach, but something I wasn't so adept at, since the children, at least the most forward of them, immediately discovered how uncomfortable I was in their presence.

Oh, how undignified this was!

Everything was suddenly turned on its head. I, who wasn't fond of the nursery Vanja attended, who just wanted it to look after Vanja for me so that I could work in peace for some hours every day without knowing what she was doing or how she was, I who didn't want any closeness in my life, who could not get enough of distance, could not be alone enough, who all of a sudden had to spend a week there as an employee and get involved in everything that happened, but it did not stop there, for when you dropped off your children or picked them up it was normal to sit for a few minutes in the playroom or dining room or wherever they were, and chat to the other parents, perhaps play a little with the children, and every day of the week . . . I usually kept this to the bare minimum, took Vanja and put on her coat before anyone discovered what was going on, but now and then I was trapped in the corridor, a conversation was initiated, and, hey presto, there I was sitting on one of those low deep sofas making agreement noises about something or other that was of no interest to me whatsoever while the brashest of the children yanked and tugged at me, wanting me to throw them, carry them, swing them round or, in the case of Jocke, who incidentally was the son of the kind book-loving banker Gustav, was content merely to stab me with sharp objects.

Spending Saturday afternoon and evening squeezed between others at a table and eating vegetables with a strained but courteous smile on your face was part of the same obligation.

Erik lifted down a stack of plates from a cupboard above the worktop while Frida counted knives and forks. I took a sip of wine and could feel how hungry I was. Stella stopped in the doorway, her face red and a little sweaty.

'Is it time for the cake now?' she called.

Frida swivelled round.

'Soon, sweetheart. But first we have to eat some proper food.'

Her attention wandered from the child to those sitting around the table.

'The food's ready,' she said. 'Help yourselves. There are the plates and cutlery. And you can take some food for your children too.'

'Ah, that sounds good,' Linus said, getting up. 'What is there?'

I had planned to stay seated until the queue had died down. When I saw what Linus had returned with – beans, salad, the ever-present couscous and a hot dish I assumed was chickpea casserole – I got up and went into the kitchen.

'Food's in there,' I said to Linda, who was standing with Vanja wrapped around her legs and Heidi in her arms chatting to Mia. 'Shall we swap?'

'Yes, that's good,' Linda said. 'I'm ravenous.'

'Can we go home now, daddy?' Vanja said.

'But we're eating,' I said. 'And afterwards there's cake. Shall I get you some food?'

'Don't want anything,' she said.

'I'll get you something anyway,' I said, and took Heidi by the arm. 'And you come with me.'

'Heidi's had a banana, by the way,' Linda said. 'But she'll probably want some food as well.'

'Come on, Theresa, let's go and get something for you,' Mia said.

I followed them in, lifted Heidi into my arms and stood in the queue. She rested her head against my shoulder, which she only did when she was tired. My shirt stuck to my chest. Every face I saw, every glance I met, every voice I heard, hung like a lead weight on me. When I was asked a question, or asked a question myself, it was as if the words had to be dynamited out. Heidi made it easier, having her there was a kind of protection, both because I had something to occupy myself with and because her presence diverted others' attention. They smiled at her, asked if she was tired and stroked her cheek. A large part of my relationship with Heidi was based on me carrying her. It was the basis of our relationship. She always wanted to be carried, never wanted to walk, stretched up her arms as soon as she saw me, and smiled with pleasure whenever she was allowed to hang from my arms. And I liked having her close, the little chubby creature with the greedy mouth.

I put some beans, a couple of spoonfuls of chickpea casserole and a dollop of couscous on a plate and carried it into the living room, where all the children were sitting around the low table in the middle, with a helpful parent behind.

'Don't want anything,' Vanja said as soon as I set the plate in front of her.

'That's OK,' I said. 'You don't have to eat if you don't want to. But do you think Heidi wants some?'

I speared some beans on the fork and raised it to her mouth. She pinched her lips together and twisted her head away.

'Come on now,' I said. 'I know you're both hungry.'

'Can we play with the train?' Vanja asked.

I looked at her. Normally she would have stared either at the train set or up at me, begging as often as not, but now she was staring straight ahead.

'Of course we can,' I said. I put Heidi down and went to the corner of the room where I had to press my knees against my body, almost into my chest, to make room between the tiny children's furniture and the toy boxes. I took the railway track apart and passed it piece by piece to Vanja, who tried to reassemble it. When the pieces didn't fit she forced them together with all her strength. I waited until she was on the point of throwing them down in fury before intervening. Heidi constantly wanted to tear the track up, and my eyes searched for something to give her as a diversion. A puzzle? A cuddly toy? A little plastic pony with large eyelashes and a long pink synthetic mane? She hurled all of them away.

'Daddy, can you help me?' Vanja said.

'Course I can,' I said. 'Look. Let's put a bridge here, so the train can go over and under it. That'll be good, won't it.'

Heidi grabbed one of the bridge pieces.

'Heidi!' Vanja said.

I took it from her, and she began to scream. I took her in my arms and stood up.

'I can't do it!' Vanja said.

'I'll be there in a sec. I'm just going to take Heidi to mummy,' I said, and went to the kitchen carrying Heidi on my hip like an experienced housewife. Linda was chatting with Gustav, the only one of the Lodjuret parents with a good old-fashioned profession, and with whom for some reason she got on well. He was jovial, his face shone, his short always neatly dressed body was robust and stocky, his neck strong, his chin broad, his face chubby but open and cheerful. He liked talking about books he had enjoyed, the latest of which were by Richard Ford.

'They're fantastic,' he would say. 'Have you read them? They're about an estate agent, an ordinary man, yes, and his life, so recognisable and normal. Ford captures the whole spirit of America! The American mood, the very pulse of the country!'

I liked Gustav, especially his decency, which was thanks to nothing more complicated than his having a basic, honest job, which incidentally none of my friends had, least of all myself. We were the same age, but I thought of him as ten years older from his appearance. He was adult in the way our parents had been when I was growing up.

'I think perhaps Heidi ought to go to sleep soon,' I said. 'She seems tired. And probably hungry too. Will you take her home?'

'Yes, just have to finish eating first, OK?'

'Of course.'

'Now I've held your book in my hand!' Gustav said. 'I was in the bookshop, and there it was. It looked interesting. Was it published by Norstedts?'

'Yes,' I said with a strained smile. 'It was.'

'You didn't buy it then?' Linda asked, not without a teasing tone to her voice.

'No, not this time,' he said, wiping his mouth with a serviette. 'It's about angels, isn't it?'

I nodded. Heidi had slipped from my grasp, and when I lifted her up again I noticed how heavy her nappy was.

'I'll change her before you go,' I said. 'You brought the changing bag, didn't you?'

'Yes, it's in the hall.'

'OK,' I said, and went out to fetch a nappy. In the living

room Vanja and Achilles were running around, jumping from the sofa onto the floor, laughing, getting up and jumping off again. I felt a surge of warmth in my breast. Leaned over and picked up a nappy and a packet of wipes while Heidi clung to me like a little koala bear. There was no changing table in the bathroom, so I laid her on the floor tiles, took off her stockings, tore off the two adhesive tabs on the nappy and threw it in the bin under the sink while Heidi watched me with a serious expression.

'Just wee-wee!' she said. Then she turned her head to the side and stared at the wall, apparently unmoved by my putting on a clean nappy, the way she had done ever since she was a baby.

'There we are,' I said. 'That's you done.'

I grabbed her hands and pulled her up. Then folded her tights, which were slightly damp, and took them to the bag on the buggy, whereupon I dressed her in some jogging pants I found, and then the brown bubble-lined corduroy jacket she had been given for her first birthday by Yngve. Linda came in while I was putting on Heidi's shoes.

'I'll be coming soon too,' I said. We kissed, Linda took the bag in one hand, Heidi in the other, and they left.

Vanja ran at top speed down the hallway, with Achilles in tow, into what must have been the bedroom, from where her overexcited voice could be heard soon afterwards. The thought of going in and sitting at the kitchen table again was not exactly appealing, so I opened the bathroom door, locked it behind me and stood there motionless for a few

minutes. Then washed my face in cold water, dried it carefully on a white towel and met my eyes in the mirror, so
dark and in a face so rigid with frustration I almost started
with alarm at the sight.

No one in the kitchen noticed that I was back. Except
for a stern-looking little woman with short hair and ordinary angular features, who stared for a brief moment at me
from behind her glasses. What did she want now?

Gustav and Linus were discussing pension arrange-
ments, the taciturn man with the 50s shirt had his child, a
wild boy with blond, almost white hair, on his lap, and was
discussing FC Malmö with him, while Frida chatted with
Mia about club evenings she and some friends were going
to start. Meanwhile, Erik and Mathias compared TV screens,
a discussion which Linus wanted to join, I could see that
from his long glances and the shorter ones to Gustav so as
not to appear impolite. The only person not deep in conversation was the woman with cropped hair, and even though
I looked in every direction apart from hers she still leaned
across the table and asked if I was satisfied with the nursery.
I said I was. There was perhaps a bit too much to do there,
I added, but it was definitely worth the investment of time;
you got to know your children's playmates, and that could
only be good, I opined.

She smiled at what I said without any great fervour.
There was something sad about her, some unhappiness.

'What the hell?' Linus said suddenly, thrusting his chair
back. 'What are they *doing* in there?'

He got up and went to the bathroom. The next moment he came out with Vanja and Achilles in front of him. Vanja had put on her broadest smile, Achilles looked rather more guilt-ridden. The sleeves of his small suit jacket were soaked. Vanja's bare arms glistened with moisture.

'They had their hands as far down the toilet as they could get them when I went in,' Linus said. I met Vanja's eyes and couldn't help smiling.

'We'll have to take this off now, young man,' Linus said, leading Achilles into the hall. 'And you make sure you wash your hands properly.'

'The same applies to you, Vanja,' I said, getting up. 'Into the bathroom with you.'

She stretched out her arms over the basin and looked up at me.

'I'm playing with Achilles!' she said.

'I can see that,' I said. 'But you don't have to stick your hands down the loo to do that, do you?'

'No,' she said, and laughed.

I wetted my hands under the tap, soaped them, and washed her arms from the tips of her fingers to her shoulders. Then I dried them before kissing her on the forehead and sending her out again. The apologetic smile I wore when I sat down was unnecessary, no one was interested in pursuing this little episode, not even Linus, who as soon as he returned continued the story about a man he had seen attacked by monkeys in Thailand. His face didn't even break into a smile when the others laughed, but he seemed to inhale their laughter, as if to give the story renewed vigour, which it did, and only when the next wave of laughter broke did he smile, not much, and not at his own wit, it struck me; it was more like an expression of the satisfaction he felt when his face could bask in the merriment he had evoked. 'Yeah, yeah, yeah,' he said, jabbing his hand in the air. The stern woman, who thus far had been looking out of the window, pulled her chair up and leaned across the table again.

'Isn't it tough to have two children so close in age?' she asked.

'Yes and no,' I answered. 'It is a bit wearing. But it's still better with two than one. The single-child scenario seems a bit sad, if you ask me . . . I've always thought I wanted to have three children. Then there are lots of permutations when they play. And the children are in the majority vis-à-vis the parents . . .'

I smiled. She said nothing. All of a sudden I realised she had an only child.

'But just one can be brilliant too,' I said.

She rested her head on her hand.

'But I wish Gustav had a brother or a sister,' she said. 'It's too much with just us two.'

'Not at all,' I said. 'He'll have loads of pals in the nursery, and that's great.'

'The problem is I haven't got a husband,' she said. 'And so it's not possible.'

What the *fuck* had that got to do with me?

I sent her a look of sympathy and concentrated on preventing my eyes from wandering, which can easily happen in such situations.

'And I can't imagine the men I meet as fathers to my children,' she continued.

'Nonsense,' I said. 'These things sort themselves out.'

'I don't believe they do,' she said. 'But thank you anyway.'

From the corner of my eye I detected a movement. I turned and looked towards the door. Vanja was coming my way. She stopped right next to me.

'I want to go home,' she said. 'Can't we go now?'

'We have to stay for a just a little longer,' I said. 'Soon there'll be cake too. You want some of that, don't you?'

She didn't answer.

'Do you want to sit on my lap?' I asked.

She nodded, and I moved my wine glass and lifted her up.

'You sit with me for a bit, and then we'll go back in. I can stay with you. OK?'

'OK.'

She sat watching the others round the table. I wondered what she was thinking. How did it seem to her?

I observed her. Her blonde hair was already over her shoulders. A small nose, a little mouth, two tiny ears, both with pointed elfin tips. Her blue eyes, which always betrayed her mood, had a slight squint, hence the glasses. At first she had been proud of them. Now they were the first thing she took off when she was angry. Perhaps because she knew it was important for us that she should wear them?

With us her eyes were lively and cheerful, that is if they didn't lock and become unapproachable when she was having one of her grand bouts of fury. She was hugely dramatic and could rule the whole family with her temperament; she performed large-scale and complicated relational dramas with her toys, loved having stories read to her but watching films even more, and then preferably ones with characters and high drama which she puzzled over and discussed with us, bursting with questions but also the joy of retelling. For a period it was Astrid Lindgren's character Madicken she was mad about, and this caused her to jump off the chairs and lie on the floor with her eyes closed; we had to lift her and think at first that she was dead, then realise she had fainted and had concussion, before carrying her, with eyes closed and arms hanging down, to her bed, where she was to lie for three days, preferably while we hummed the sad theme from this scene in the film. Then she leaped to her feet, ran to the chair and started all over again. At the nursery's Christmas party she was the only one who bowed in response to the applause and who obviously enjoyed the attention. Often the idea of something meant more to her than the thing itself, such as with sweets; she could talk about them for an entire day and look forward to them, but when the sweets were in the bowl in front of her she barely tasted one before spitting it out. However, she didn't learn from the experience: the next Saturday her expectations of the fantastic sweets were as high again. She wanted so much to go skating, but when we were there, at the rink, with the small skates Linda's mother had bought for her on her feet and the little ice hockey helmet on her head, she shrieked with anger at the realisation that she couldn't keep her balance and probably wouldn't learn to do so any time soon. All the greater therefore was her joy at seeing that she could in fact ski, which happened once when we were on the small patch of snow in my mother's garden trying out equipment she had come by. But then too the idea of skiing and the joy at being able to do it were greater than actually skiing; she could function quite happily without that. She loved to travel with us, loved to see new places and talked about all the things that had happened for several months afterwards. But most of all she loved to play with other children, of course. It was a great experience for her when other children at the nursery came back home with her. The first time Benjamin was due to come she went around the evening before, inspecting her toys, worried stiff that they were not good enough for him. She had just turned three. But when he arrived they got on like a house on fire and all prior concerns went up in a whirl of excitement and euphoria. Benjamin told his parents that Vanja was the nicest girl in the nursery, and when I told her that – she was sitting in bed playing with her Barbies – she reacted with a display of emotion she had never manifested before.

'Do you know what Benjamin said?' I said from the doorway.

'No,' she said, looking up at me with sudden interest.

'He said you were the nicest girl in the nursery.'

I had never seen her filled with such light. She was glowing with happiness. I knew that neither Linda nor I would be able to say anything to make her react like that, and I understood with the immediate clarity of an insight that she was not ours. Her life was utterly her own.

'What did he say?' she answered, she wanted to hear it again.

'He said you were the nicest in the nursery.'

Her smile was shy but happy, and that made me glad too, yet a shadow hung over my happiness, for was it not alarmingly early for others' thoughts and opinions to mean so much to her? Wasn't it best for everything to come from her, for it to be rooted in herself? Another time she surprised me like this was when I was in the nursery. I had gone to pick her up and she ran towards me in the corridor and asked if Stella could go with her to the stables afterwards. I said that things didn't work like that, it had to be planned in advance, we had to speak to her parents first, and Vanja stood watching me say this, obviously disappointed, but when she went to pass on the news to Stella, she didn't use my reasons. I heard her as I was rummaging in the hall for her rain gear.

'It'll be a bit boring for you at the stables,' she said. 'Just watching isn't cool.'

This way of thinking, putting others' reactions before your own, I recognised from myself, and as we walked towards Folkets Park in the rain I wondered about how she had picked that up. Was it just there, around her, invisible but present, like the air she breathed? Or was it genetic?

I never expressed any of these thoughts I had about the children, except to Linda of course, because these complex questions belonged only where they were, in me and between us. In reality, in the world Vanja inhabited everything was simple and found simple expression, and the complexity arose only in the sum of all the parts, of which naturally she knew nothing. And the fact that we talked a lot about them did not help at all in our daily lives, where everything was a mess and constantly on the verge of chaos. In the first of the Swedish 'progress conversations' we had with the nursery staff there was a lot of talk about her not making contact with the teachers, not wanting to sit on their laps or be patted, as well as her shyness. We should work on toughening her up, teaching her to play a more dominant role in games, taking the initiative and talking more, they said. Linda replied that she was tough enough at home, took the lead in all the games, always showed initiative and could talk the hind leg off a donkey. They told us the little she said in the nursery was unclear, her Swedish wasn't correct, her vocabulary was not that large, so they were wondering if we had considered speech therapy. At this juncture in the conversation we were handed a brochure from one of the town's speech therapists. They are crazy in this country, I thought. A speech therapist? Did everything have to be institutionalised? She's only three!

'No, speech therapy's out of the question,' I said. Until that point Linda had been the one to do all the talking. 'It will sort itself out. I only *started* talking when I was three. Before that I said nothing, apart from single words which were incomprehensible to anyone except my brother.'

They smiled.

'And when I started speaking it came in long, fluent sentences. It all depends on the individual. We are not sending her to a speech therapist.'

'Well, that's up to you,' said Olaf, the head of the nursery. 'But you're welcome to hang on to the brochures and give it some thought.'

'OK then,' I said.

When I was with other people I was bound to them, the nearness I felt was immense, the empathy great. Indeed, so great that their well-being was always more important than my own. I subordinated myself, almost to the verge of self-effacement; some uncontrollable internal mechanism caused me to put their thoughts and opinions before my own. But the moment I was alone others meant nothing to me. It wasn't that I disliked them, or nurtured feelings of loathing for them; on the contrary, I liked most of them, and the ones I didn't actually like I could always see some worth in, some attribute I could identify with, or at least find interesting, something which could occupy my mind for the moment. But liking them was not the same as caring about them. It was the social situation that bound me, the people within it did not. Between these two perspectives there was no halfway house. There was just the small self-effacing one and the large distance-creating one. And in between them was where my daily life lay. Perhaps that was why I had such a hard time living it. Everyday life, with its duties and routines, was something I endured, not a thing I enjoyed, nor something that was meaningful or made me happy. This had nothing to do with a lack of desire to wash floors or change nappies but rather with something more fundamental: the life around me was not meaningful. I always longed to be away from it, and always had done. So the life I led was not my own. I tried to make it mine, this was my struggle, because of course I wanted it, but I failed, the longing for something else undermined all my efforts.

What was the problem?

Was it the shrill sickly tone I heard everywhere, which I couldn't stand, the one that arose from all the pseudo people and pseudo places, pseudo events and pseudo conflicts our lives passed through, that which we saw but did not participate in, and the distance that modern life in this way had opened up to our own, actually inalienable, here and now? If so, if it was more reality, more involvement I longed for, surely I should be embracing that which I was surrounded by? And not, as was the case, longing to get away from it? Or perhaps it was the prefabricated nature of the days in this world I was reacting to, the rails of routine we followed, which made everything so predictable that we had to invest in entertainment to feel any hint of intensity? Every time I went out of the door I knew what was going to happen, what I was going to do. This was how it was on the micro level, I go to the supermarket and do the shopping, I go and sit down at a café with a newspaper, I fetch my children from the nursery, and this is how it was on the macro level, from the initial entry into society, the nursery, to the final exit, the old folks' home. Or was the revulsion I felt based on the sameness that was spreading through the world and making everything smaller? If you travelled through Norway now you saw the same everywhere. The same roads, the same houses, the same petrol stations, the same shops. As late as in the 60s you could see how local culture changed as you drove through Gudbrandsdalen, for example, the strange black timber buildings, so pure and sombre, which were now encapsulated as small museums in a culture which was no different from the one you had left or the one you were going to. And Europe, which was merging more and more into one large, homogeneous country. The same, the same, everything was the same. Or was it perhaps that the light which illuminated the world and made everything comprehensible also drained it of meaning? Was it perhaps the forests that had vanished, the animal species that had become extinct, the ways of life that would never return?

Yes, all of this I thought about, all of this filled me with sorrow and a sense of helplessness, and if there was a world I turned to in my mind, it was that of the sixteenth and seventeenth centuries, with its enormous forests, its sailing ships and horse-drawn carts, its windmills and castles, its monasteries and small towns, its painters and thinkers, explorers and inventors, priests and alchemists. What would it have been like to live in a world where everything was made from the power of your hands, the wind or the water? What would it have been like to live in a world where the American Indians still lived their lives in peace? Where that life was an actual possibility? Where Africa was unconquered? Where darkness came with the sunset and light with the sunrise? Where there were too few humans and their tools were too rudimentary to have any effect on animal stocks, let alone wipe them out? Where you could not travel from one place to another without exerting yourself, and a comfortable life was something only the rich could afford, where the sea was full of whales, the forests full of bears and wolves, and there were still countries that were so alien no adventure story could do them justice, such as China, to which a voyage not only took several months and was the prerogative of only a tiny minority of sailors and traders, but was also fraught with danger. Admittedly, that world was rough and wretched, filthy and ravaged with sickness, drunken and ignorant, full of pain, low life expectancy and rampant superstition, but it produced the greatest writer, Shakespeare, the greatest painter, Rembrandt, the greatest scientist, Newton, all still unsurpassed in their fields, and how can it be that this period achieved this wealth? Was it because death was closer and life was starker as a result?

Who knows?

Be that as it may, we can't go back in time, everything we undertake is irrevocable, and if we look back what we see is not life but death. And whoever believes that the conditions and character of the times are responsible for our maladjustment is either suffering from delusions of grandeur or is simply stupid, and lacks self-knowledge on both accounts. I loathed so much about the age I lived in, but it was not that that was the cause of the loss of meaning, because it was not something that had been constant . . . The spring I moved to Stockholm and met Linda, for example, the world had suddenly opened, the intensity in it increased at breakneck speed. I was head over heels in love and everything was possible, my happiness was at bursting point all the time and embraced everything. If someone had spoken to me then about a lack of meaning I would have laughed out loud, for I was free and the world lay at my feet, open, packed with meaning, from the gleaming futuristic trains that streaked across Slussen beneath my flat, to the sun colouring the nineteenth-century-style church spires in Ridderholmen red, sinisterly beautiful sunsets I witnessed every evening for all those months, from the aroma of freshly picked basil and the taste of ripe tomatoes to the sound of clacking heels on the cobbled slope down to the Hilton hotel late one night when we sat on a bench holding hands and knowing that it would be us two now and for ever. This state lasted for six months, for six months I was truly happy, truly at home in this world and in myself before slowly it began to lose its lustre, and once more the world moved out of my reach. One year later it happened again, if in quite a different way. That was when Vanja was born. Then it was not the world which opened – we had shut it out, in a kind of total concentration on the miracle taking place in our midst – no, something opened in me. While falling in love had been wild and abandoned, brimming with life and exuberance, this was cautious and muted, filled with endless attention to what was happening. Four weeks, maybe five, it lasted. Whenever I had to do some shopping in town I *ran* down the streets, grabbed whatever we needed, shook with impatience at the counter, and *ran* back with the bags hanging from my hands. I didn't want to miss a minute! The days and nights merged into one, everything was tenderness, everything was gentleness, and if she opened her eyes we rushed towards her. Oh, there you are! But that passed too, we got used to that too, and I began to work, sat in my new office in Dalagatan writing every day while Linda was at home with Vanja and came to see me for lunch, often worried about something but also happy, she was closer to the child and what was happening than me, for I was writing, what had started out as a long essay slowly but surely was growing into a novel, it soon reached a point where it was everything, and writing was all I did, I moved into the office, wrote day and night, sleeping an hour here and

The days and nights merged into one, everything was tenderness, everything was gentleness, and if she opened her eyes we rushed towards her. Oh, there you are!

there. I was filled with an absolutely fantastic feeling, a kind of light burned within me, not hot and consuming but cold and clear and shining. At night I took a cup of coffee with me and sat down on the bench outside the hospital to smoke, the streets around me were quiet, and I could hardly sit still, so great was my happiness. Everything was possible, everything made sense. At two places in the novel I soared higher than I had thought possible, and those two places alone, which I could not believe I had written, and no one else has noticed or said anything about, made the preceding five years of failed writing worth all the effort. They are two of the best moments in my life. By which I mean my whole life. The happiness that filled me and the feeling of invincibility they gave me I have searched for ever since, in vain.

A few weeks after the novel was finished life began as a house husband, and the plan was it would last until next spring while Linda did the last year of her training at the Dramatiska Institut. The novel writing had taken its toll on our relationship. I slept in the office for six weeks, barely seeing Linda and our five-month-old daughter, and when at last it was over she was relieved and happy, and I owed it to her to be there, not just in the same room, physically, but also with all my attention and participation. I couldn't do it. For several months I felt a sorrow at not being where I had been, in the cold clear environment, and my yearning to return was stronger than my pleasure at the life we lived. The fact that the novel was doing well didn't matter. After every good review I put a cross in the book and waited for the next, after every conversation with the agent at the publisher's, when a foreign company had shown some interest or made an offer, I put a cross in my book and waited for the next, and I wasn't very interested when it was eventually nominated for the Nordic Council Literature Prize, for if there was one thing I had learned over the last six months it was that all writing was about *writing*. Therein lay all its value. Yet I wanted to have more of what came in its wake because public attention is a drug, the need it satisfies is artificial, but once you have had a taste of it you want more. So there I was, pushing the buggy on my endless walks on the island of Djurgården in Stockholm waiting for the telephone to ring and a journalist to ask me about something, an event organiser to invite me somewhere, a magazine to ask for an article, a publisher to make an offer, until at last I took the consequences of the disagreeable taste it left in my mouth and began to say no to everything at the same time as the interest ebbed away and I was back to the everyday grind. But no matter how hard I tried, I couldn't get into it, there was always something else that was more important. Vanja sat there in the buggy looking around while I trudged through the town, first here, then there, or sat in the sandpit digging with a spade in the play area in Humlegården, where the tall lean Stockholm mothers who surrounded us were constantly on their phones, looking as if they were part of some bloody fashion show, or she was in her high chair in the kitchen at home swallowing the food I fed her. All of this bored me out of my mind. I felt stupid walking round indoors chatting to her, because she didn't say anything; there was just my inane voice and her silence, happy babbling or displeased tears, then it was on with her clothes and tramping into town again, to the Moderna Museet in Skeppsholmen, for example, where at least I could see some good art while keeping an eye on her, or to one of the big bookshops in the centre, or to Djurgården or Brunnsviken Lake, which was the closest the town came to nature, unless I took the road out to see Geir, who had his office in the university at that time. Little by little, I mastered everything with regard to small children, there wasn't a single thing I couldn't do with her, we were everywhere, but no matter how well it went, and irrespective of the great tenderness I felt for her, my boredom and apathy were greater. A lot of effort was spent getting her to sleep so that I could read and to making the days pass so that I could cross them off in the calendar. I got to know the most out-of-the-way cafés in town, and there was hardly a park bench I had not sat on at some time or other, with a book in one hand and the buggy in the other. I took Dostoevsky with me, first *Demons*, then *The Brothers Karamazov*. In them I found the light again. But it wasn't the lofty, clear and pure light, as with Hölderlin; with Dostoevsky there were no heights, no mountains, there was no divine perspective, everything was in the human domain, wreathed in this characteristically Dostoevskian wretched, dirty, sick, almost contaminated mood

No matter how well it went, and irrespective of the great tenderness I felt for her, my boredom and apathy were greater that was never too far from hysteria. That was where the light was. That was where the divine stirred. But was this the place to go? Was it necessary to go down on bended knee? As usual I didn't think as I read, just engrossed myself in it, and after a few hundred pages, which took several days to read, something suddenly happened: all the details that had been painstakingly built up slowly began to interact, and the intensity was so great that I was carried along, totally enthralled, until Vanja opened her eyes from the depths of the buggy, almost suspicious, it seemed: where have you taken me now?

There was no option but to close the book, lift her up, get out the spoon, the jar of food and the bib if we were indoors, set a course for the nearest café if we were outside, fetch a high chair, put her in it and go over to the counter and ask the staff to warm the food, which they did grudgingly because Stockholm was inundated with babies at that time, there was a baby boom, and since there were so many women in their thirties among the mothers who had worked and led their own lives until then, glamorous magazines for mothers began to appear, with children as a sort of accessory, and one celebrity after another allowed herself to be photographed with and interviewed about her family. What had previously taken place in private was now pumped into the public arena. Everywhere you could read about labour pains, Caesareans and breastfeeding, baby clothes, buggies and holiday tips for parents of small children, published in books written by house husbands or bitter mothers who felt cheated as they collapsed with exhaustion from working and having children. What had once been normal topics you didn't talk about much were now placed at the forefront of existence and cultivated with a frenzy that ought to make everyone raise their eyebrows, for what could be the meaning of this? In the midst of this lunacy there was me trundling my child around like one of the many fathers who had evidently put fatherhood before all else. When I was in the café feeding Vanja there was always at least one other father there, usually of my age, that is, in his mid-thirties, almost all of whom had shaved heads to hide hair loss. You hardly ever saw a bald patch or a high forehead any longer, and the sight of these fathers always made me feel a little uncomfortable. I found it hard to take the feminised aspect of their actions, even though I did exactly the same and was as feminised as they were. The slight disdain I felt for men pushing buggies was, to put it mildly, a two-edged sword as for the most part I had one in front of me when I saw them. I doubted I was alone in these feelings, I thought I could occasionally discern an uneasy look on some men's faces in the play area, and the restlessness in the bodies, which were prone to snatching a couple of pull-ups on the bars while the children played around them. However, spending a few hours every day in a play area with your child was one thing. There were things that were much worse. Linda had just started to take Vanja to Rhythm Time classes for tiny tots at the Stadsbiblioteket library, and when I took over responsibility she wanted

Vanja to continue. I had an inkling something dreadful was awaiting me, so I said no, it was out of the question, Vanja was with me now, so there would be no Rhythm Time. But Linda continued to mention it off and on, and after a few months my resistance to what the role of the soft man involved was so radically subverted, in addition to which Vanja had grown so much that her day needed a modicum of variety, that one day I said, yes, today we were thinking of going to the Rhythm Time course at the Stadsbiblioteket. Remember to get there in good time, Linda said, it fills up quickly. And so it was that early one afternoon I was pushing Vanja up Sveavägen to Odenplan, where I crossed the road and went through the library doors. For some reason I had never been there before, even though it was one of Stockholm's most beautiful buildings, designed by Asplund some time in the 1920s, the period I liked best of all in the previous century. Vanja was fed, rested and wearing clean clothes, carefully chosen for the occasion. I pushed the buggy into the large completely circular interior, asked a woman behind a counter where the children's section was, followed her instructions into a side room lined with shelves of children's books, where on a door at the back there was a poster about this Rhythm Time class starting here at 2 p.m. Three buggies were already present. On some chairs a little further away sat the owners, three women in heavy jackets and worn faces, all around thirty-five, while what must have been their snot-nosed children were crawling around on the floor between them.

I parked the buggy by theirs, lifted Vanja out, sat down on a little ledge with her on my lap, removed her jacket and shoes and lowered her gently to the floor. Reckoned she could crawl around a bit as well. But she didn't want to, she couldn't remember being here before, so she wanted to stick with me and stretched her arms out. I lifted her back onto my lap. She sat watching the other children with interest.

An attractive young woman holding a guitar walked across the floor. She must have been about twenty-five; she had long blonde hair, a coat reaching down to her knees, high black boots and she stopped in front of me.

'Hi!' she said. 'Haven't seen you here before. Are you coming to the Rhythm Time class?'

'Yes,' I said, looking up at her. She really was attractive.

'Have you signed up?'

'No,' I said. 'Do you have to?'

'Yes, you do. And I'm afraid it's full today.'

Good news.

'What a shame,' I said, getting up.

'As you didn't know,' she said. 'I suppose we can squeeze you in. Just this once. You can sign up afterwards for the next time.'

'Thank you,' I said.

Her smile was so attractive. Then she opened the door and went in. I leaned forward and watched her putting her guitar case on the floor, removing her coat and scarf and hanging them over a chair at the back of the room. She had a light fresh spring-like presence.

I had a hunch where this was going, and I should have got up and left. But I wasn't there for my sake, I was there for Vanja and Linda. So I stayed put. Vanja was eight months old and absolutely bewitched by anything that resembled a performance. And now she was attending one.

More women with buggies came, in dribs and drabs, and soon the room was filled with the sounds of chatting, coughing, laughing, clothes rustling and rummaging through bags. Most seemed to come in twos or threes. For a long time I seemed to be the only person on my own. But just before two a couple more men arrived. From their body language I could see they didn't know each other. One of them, a small guy with a big head, wearing glasses, nodded to me. I could have kicked him. What did he think: that we belonged to the same club? Then it was off with the overalls, the hat and the shoes, out with the feeding bottle and rattle, down on the floor with the child.

The mothers had long since gone into the room where Rhythm Time was due to take place. I waited until last, but at a minute to, I got up and went in with Vanja on my arm. Cushions had been strewn across the floor for us to sit on, while the young woman leading the session sat on a chair in front of us. With the guitar on her lap she scanned the audience smiling. She was wearing a beige cashmere jumper. Her breasts were well formed, her waist was narrow, her legs, one crossed over the other and swinging, were long and still clad in black boots.

I sat down on my cushion. I put Vanja on my lap. She

stared with big eyes at the woman with the guitar, who was now saying a few words of welcome.

'We've got some new faces here today,' she said. 'Perhaps you'd like to introduce yourselves?'

'Monica,' said one.

'Kristina,' said another.

'Lul,' said a third.

Lul? What sort of bloody name was that?

The room went quiet. The attractive young woman looked at me and sent me a smile of encouragement.

'Karl Ove,' I said sombrely.

'Then let's start with our welcome song,' she said, and struck the first chord, which resounded as she was explaining that parents should say the name of their child when she nodded to them, and then everyone should sing the child's name.

She strummed the same chord, and everyone began to sing. The idea behind the song was that everyone should say 'Hi' to their friend and wave a hand. Parents of the children too small to understand took their wrists and waved their hands, which I did too, but when the second verse started I no longer had any excuse for sitting there in silence and had to start singing. My own deep voice sounded like an affliction in the choir of high-pitched women's voices. Twelve times we sang 'Hi' to our friend before all the children had been named and we could move on. The next song was about parts of the body, which, of course, the children should touch when they were mentioned. Forehead, eyes, ears, nose, mouth, stomach, knee, foot. Forehead, eyes, ears, nose, mouth, stomach, knee, foot. Then we were handed some rattle-like instruments which we were supposed to shake as we sang a new song. I wasn't embarrassed, it wasn't embarrassing sitting there, it was humiliating and degrading. Everything was gentle and friendly and nice, all the movements were tiny, and I sat huddled on a cushion droning along with the mothers and children, a song, to cap it all, led by a woman I would have liked to bed. But sitting there I was rendered completely harmless, without dignity, impotent, there was no difference between me and her, except that she was more attractive, and the levelling, whereby I had forfeited everything that was me, even my size, and that voluntarily, filled me with rage.

'Now it's time for the children to do a bit of dancing!' she said, laying her guitar on the floor. Then she got up and went to a CD player on a chair.

'Everyone stand in a ring, and first we go one way, stamp with our feet, like so,' she said, stamping her attractive foot, 'turn round once and go back the other way.'

I got up, lifted Vanja and stood in the circle that was forming. I looked for the other two men. Both were completely focused on their children.

'OK, OK, Vanja,' I whispered. '"Each to his own," as your great-grandfather used to say.'

She looked up at me. So far she hadn't shown any interest in any of the things the children had to do. She didn't even want to shake the maracas.

'Away we go, then,' said the attractive woman, pressing the CD player. A folk tune poured into the room, and I began to follow the others, each step in time to the music. I held Vanja with a hand under each arm, so that she was dangling, close to my chest. Then what I had to do was stamp my foot, swing her round, after which it was back the other way. Lots of the others enjoyed this, there was laughter and even some squeals of delight. When this was over we had to dance alone with our child. I swayed from side to side with Vanja in my arms thinking that this must be what hell was like, gentle and nice and full of mothers you didn't know from Eve with their babies. When this was finished there was a session with a large blue sail which at first was supposed to be the sea, and we sang a song about waves and everyone swung the sail up and down, making waves, and then it was something the children had to crawl under until we suddenly raised it, this too to the accompaniment of our singing.

When at last she thanked us and said goodbye, I hurried out, dressed Vanja without meeting anyone's eye, just staring down at the floor, while the voices, happier now than before they went in, buzzed around me. I put Vanja in the buggy, strapped her in and pushed her out as fast as I could without drawing attention to myself. Outside on the street I felt like shouting till my lungs burst and smashing something. But I had to make do with putting as many metres between me and this hall of shame in the shortest possible time.

'Vanja, O Vanja,' I said, scurrying down Sveavägen. 'Did you have fun then? It didn't really look like it.'

'Tha tha thaa,' Vanja said.

She didn't smile, but her eyes were happy.

She pointed.

'Ah, a motorbike,' I said. 'What is it with you and motor-bikes, eh?'

When we reached the Konsum shop at the corner of Tegnérgatan I went in to buy something for supper. The feeling of claustrophobia was still there, but the aggression had diminished, it wasn't anger I felt as I pushed the buggy down the aisle between the shelves. The shop evoked memories, it was the one I had used when I had moved to Stockholm three years earlier, when I was staying at the flat Norstedts, the publishers, had put at my disposal a stone's throw further up the street. I had weighed over a hundred kilos at the time and moved in a semi-catatonic darkness, escaping from my former life. It hadn't been much fun. But I had decided to pick myself up, so every evening I went to the Lill-Jansskogen forest to run. I couldn't even manage a hundred metres before my heart was pounding so fast and my lungs were gasping so much that I had to stop. Another hundred metres and my legs were trembling. Then it was back to the hotel-like flat at walking pace for crispbread and soup. One day I had seen a woman in the shop, suddenly she was standing next to me, by the meat counter of all places, and there was some-thing about her, the sheer physicality of her appearance, which from one moment to the next filled me with almost explosive lust. She was holding her basket in front of her with both hands, her hair was auburn, her pale complexion freckled. I caught a whiff of her body, a faint smell of sweat and soap, and stood staring straight ahead with a thumping heart and constricted throat for maybe fifteen seconds, for that was the time it took her to come alongside me, take a pack of salami from the counter and go on her way. I saw her again when I was about to pay, she was at the other cash desk, and the desire, which had not gone away, welled up in me again. She put her items in her bag, turned and went out of the door. I never saw her again.

From her low position in the buggy Vanja had spotted a dog, which she was pointing a finger at. I never stopped pondering about what she saw when she watched the world around her. What did this endless stream of people, faces, cars, shops and signs mean to her? She did not see it in an undiscriminating way, that at least was certain, for not only did she regularly point at motorbikes, cats, dogs and other babies, she had also constructed a very clear hierarchy with respect to the people around her: first Linda, then me, then grandma and then everyone else, depending on how long they had been near her over the last few days.

'Yes, look, a dog,' I said. I picked up a carton of milk, which I put on the buggy, and a packet of fresh pasta from the adjacent counter. Then I took two packets of serrano ham, a jar of olives, mozzarella cheese, a pot of basil and some tomatoes. This was food I would never have dreamed of buying in my former life because I had no idea it existed. But now I was here, in the midst of Stockholm's cultural middle classes, and even though this pandering to all things Italian, Spanish, French and the repudiation of all things Swedish appeared stupid to me, and gradually, as the bigger picture emerged, also repugnant, it wasn't worth wasting my energy on. When I missed pork chops and cabbage, beef stew, vegetable soup, dumplings, meatballs, lung mash, fishcakes, mutton and vegetables, smoked sausage ring, whale steaks, sago pudding, semolina, rice pudding and Norwegian porridge, it was as much the 70s I missed as the actual tastes. And since food was not important to me, I might as well make something Linda liked.

I stopped for a few seconds by the newspaper stand wondering whether to buy the two evening papers, the two biggest publications. Reading them was like emptying a bag of rubbish over your head. Now and then I did buy them, when it felt as though a bit more rubbish up there wouldn't make any difference. But not today.

I paid and went into the street again, with the tarmac vaguely reflecting the light from the mild winter sky, and the cars queueing on all sides of the crossing resembling a huge pile-up of logs in a river. To avoid the traffic I went along Tegnérgatan. In the window of the second-hand bookshop, which was one of the ones I kept an eye on, I saw a book by Malaparte that Geir had spoken about with warmth and one by Galileo Galilei in the Atlantis series.

I turned the buggy, nudged the door open with my heel and entered backwards with the buggy following.

'I'd like two of the books in the window,' I said. 'The Galileo Galilei and the Malaparte.'

'Pardon me?' said the shirt-clad man in his fifties who ran the place, as he peered at me over the square-rimmed glasses perched on the tip of his nose.

'In the window,' I said in Swedish. 'Two books. Galilei, Malaparte.'

'The sky and the war, eh?' he said, and turned to pick them out for me.

Vanja had gone to sleep.

Had it been so exhausting at Rhythm Time?

I pulled the little lever under the headrest towards me and lowered her gently into the buggy. She waved a hand in her sleep, and clenched it exactly as she had done just after she had been born. One of the movements that nature had supplied her with but which she had slowly replaced with something of her own. But when she slept it reawakened.

I pushed the buggy to the side so that people could pass, and turned to the shelf of art books as the bookshop owner rang up the prices of the two books on his antiquated cash till. Now that Vanja was asleep I had a few more minutes to myself, and the first book I caught sight of was a photographic book by Per Maning. What luck! I had always liked his photos, especially these ones, the animal series. Cows, pigs, dogs, seals. Somehow he had succeeded in capturing their souls. There was no other way to understand the looks of these animals in the pictures. Complete presence, at times anguished, at others vacant, and sometimes penetrating. But also enigmatic, like portraits by painters in the seventeenth century.

I put it on the counter.

'That one's just come in,' the owner said. 'Fine book. Are you Norwegian?'

'Yes, I am,' I said. 'I'd like to browse a bit more if that's OK.'

There was an edition of Delacroix's diary, I took it, and then a book about Turner, even though no paintings lost as much by being photographed as his, and Poul Vad's book about Hammershøi, and a magnificent work about orientalism in art.

As I placed them on the counter my mobile rang. Almost no one had my number, so the ringtone, which found its way out of the depths of the side pocket in my parka a touch muffled, aroused no disquiet in me. Quite the contrary. Apart from the brief exchange with the Rhythm Time woman I hadn't spoken to anyone since Linda cycled to school that morning.

'Hello?' Geir said. 'What are you up to?'

'Working on my self-esteem,' I said, turning to the wall. 'And you?'

'Not that, at any rate. I'm just sitting here in the office watching everyone scurry past. So what's been happening?'

'I've just met an attractive woman.'

'And?'

'Chatted to her.'

'Mm?'

'She invited me to hers.'

'Did you say yes?'

'Of course. She even asked what my name was.'

'But?'

'She was the teacher in charge of a Rhythm Time class for babies. So I had to sit there clapping my hands and singing children's songs in front of her, with Vanja on my lap. On a little cushion. With a load of mothers and children.'

Geir burst into laughter.

'I was also given a rattle to shake.'

'Ha ha ha!'

'I was so furious when I left I didn't know what to do with myself,' I said. 'I also had a chance to try out my new waistline. And no one was bothered about the rolls of fat on my stomach.'

'No, they're nice and soft, they are,' Geir said, laughing again. 'Karl Ove, aren't we going out tonight?'

'Are you winding me up?'

'No, I'm serious. I was planning to work here till seven, more or less. So we could meet in town any time after.'

'Impossible.'

'What the hell's the point of you living in Stockholm if we can never meet?'

'You realise you just used a Swedish word, don't you,' I said.

'Can you remember when you first came to Stockholm?' Geir said. 'When you were in the taxi lecturing me about the expression "hen-pecked" when I didn't want to go to the nightclub with you?'

'There you go. And another. Your Norwegian's gone to pot,' I said.

'For Christ's sake, man. What we're talking about is the expression you used. Hen-pecked. Do you remember?'

'Yes, I'm afraid I do.'

'And?' he said. 'What do you deduce from that?'

'That there are differences,' I said. 'I'm not hen-pecked. I'm a hen-pecker. And you're a woodpecker.'

'Ha ha ha. Tomorrow then?'

'We're eating out with Fredrik and Karin tomorrow night.'

'Fredrik? Is he that idiot of a film producer?'

'I wouldn't express it in that way, but, yes, he is.'

'Oh my God. All right. Sunday? No, that's your day of rest. Monday?'

'OK.'

'There are lots of people in town then, too.'

'Monday at Pelikanen then,' I said. 'By the way, I'm holding a Malaparte book in my hand here.'

'Oh yes? Are you in a second-hand bookshop then? It's good, that one.'

'And Delacroix's diary.'

'That's supposed to be good as well. Thomas has talked about it, I know. Anything else?'

'*Aftenposten* rang yesterday. They wanted to do an interview.'

'You didn't say yes, did you?'

'Yes.'

'You idiot. You said you were going to stop doing them.'

'I know. But the publishers said the journalist was particularly good. And so I thought I would give it one last chance. It *could* turn out all right after all.'

'No, it can't,' Geir said.

'Yes, I know,' I said. 'But never mind. Now I've said yes anyway. Anything new with you?'

'Nothing. Had some bread rolls with the social anthropologists. Then the old institute head popped by with crumbs in his beard and his flies open, wanting to talk. I'm the only one who doesn't give him the heave-ho. So he comes here.'

'The one who was so tough?'

'Yes. And who's now terrified of losing his office. That's all he's got left of course. And so now he's as nice as pie. It's a question of adapting. Tough when he can be, nice when he has to be.'

'I might pop round tomorrow,' I said. 'Have you got any time?'

'Dead right I have. So long as you don't bring Vanja along, that is.'

'Ha ha. Right, but I've got to pay now. See you tomorrow.'

'OK. All the best to Linda and Vanja.'

'And to Christina.'

'See you.'

'Yes, see you.'

I rang off and stuffed the mobile back in my pocket. Vanja was still asleep. The bookshop owner was studying a catalogue. He looked up as I approached the counter.

'That'll be 1,530 kroner,' he said.

I passed him my card. I put the receipt in my back pocket – the only way I could justify these purchases of mine was that they could be written off against tax – I put the two bags of books underneath the buggy, and then I pushed it out of the shop to the sound of the doorbell ringing in my ears.

It was already twenty minutes to four. I had been up since half past four in the morning going through a problematic translation for Damm until half past six, and even though it was tedious work in which all I did was weigh one sentence against the other in the original, it was still a hundred times more interesting and rewarding than what I did during the morning in terms of nappy changing and children's activities, which for me were no longer any more than a means of occupying my time. I wasn't exhausted by this lifestyle, it had nothing to do with expending energy, but as there wasn't even the slightest spark of inspiration in it, it deflated me nonetheless, rather as if I'd had a puncture.

By the crossing at Döbelnsgatan I took a left turn, walked up the hill below Johanneskyrk, which with its red brick walls and green tin roof was similar to Johanneskirk in Bergen and Trefoldighetskirk in Arendal, followed Malmskillnadsgatan for a while, then turned down David

Bagares gata and through the gate to our backyard. Two torches were burning on the pavement outside the café opposite. There was a stench of piss, because people stopped here on their way home from Stureplan at night and pissed through the railings, and a stink of rubbish from the line of dustbins along the wall. In the corner was the pigeon that had taken up residence here when we moved in two years before. At the time it lived in a hole in the wall. When it was bricked up and sharp spikes were cemented into all the flat surfaces higher up, she moved down to ground level. There were rats here too. I saw them occasionally when I went out for a smoke at night, black backs sliding through the bushes and suddenly scuttling across the open illuminated square towards the security of the flower beds on the other side. Now one of the women hairdressers was standing there, talking on her mobile while smoking. She must have been about forty, and I guessed she had grown up as a small-town beauty, at any rate she reminded me of the type you can see in restaurants in Arendal in the summer, women in their forties with hair dyed much too blonde or much too black, skin that was much too brown, eyes much too flirtatious, laughter much too loud. Her voice was raucous, she spoke broad Skåne dialect, and today she was dressed all in white. She nodded on seeing me, and I nodded back. Even though I had barely spoken to her I liked her, she was so different from all the other people I met in Stockholm, who were either on their way up, or were up, or thought they were.

She had no truck, to put it mildly, with their homogeneous style, which not only applied to clothes and objects but also their thoughts and attitudes.

I paused in front of the door and pulled out my key. The smell of detergent and clean clothes streamed out from the vent above the cellar window. I unlocked the door and walked as quietly as I could into the hall. Vanja knew these sounds and the order in which they occurred so well that she almost always woke when we came in here. She did so this time too. With a scream. I let her scream, opened the lift door, pressed the button and regarded myself in the mirror as we went up the two floors. Linda, who must have heard the screams, was waiting for us at the door when we arrived.

'Hi,' she said. 'Have you had a good time? Have you just woken up, sweetheart? Come here then and I'll . . .'

She undid the belt and lifted Vanja up.

'We've been fine,' I said, pushing the empty buggy in while Linda unbuttoned her cardigan and went into the living room to feed her.

'But I'll never set foot in the Rhythm Time session for as long as I draw breath.'

'Was it that bad?' she asked, glancing at me with a fleeting smile before looking down at Vanja and nestling her against her bared breast.

'Bad? It's the worst experience I've ever had. I was furious when I left.'

'I see,' she said, no longer interested.

Her care for Vanja was so different. It was all-embracing. And completely genuine.

I went into the kitchen with the shopping, put the perishables in the fridge, placed the pot of basil on a dish on the windowsill and watered it, fetched the books from under the buggy and put them in the bookcase, sat down in front of the computer and checked my emails. I hadn't looked since the morning. There was an email from Carl-Johan Vallgren, he congratulated me on the nomination, said he was afraid he hadn't read my book yet, and that I just had to ring if I felt like a beer one day. Carl-Johan was someone I really liked, I valued his extravagance – which some found disagreeable, snobbish or stupid – especially after two years in Sweden. But it was impossible for me to have a beer with him. I would just sit there in silence, I knew I would; I had already done it twice. Then there was one from Marta Norheim about an interview in connection with NRK 2's Novel Award, which I had won. And one from my uncle Gunnar, who thanked me for the book and said he was building up his strength to read it, wished me luck with the Nordic championship in literature and concluded with a PS that it was a shame Yngve and Kari Anne were going to divorce. I closed the window without answering.

'Anything interesting?' Linda asked.

'Well. Carl-Johan congratulated me. And then NRK wanted to do an interview in two weeks. Gunnar wrote as well, of all people. He just thanked me for the book.

But that's not bad, considering how angry he was about *Out of the World*.'

'No, it isn't,' Linda said. 'Aren't you going to call Carl-Johan and get him to come over?'

'Are you in such a good mood?' I said.

She pouted at me.

'I'm just trying to be nice,' she said.

'I know that,' I said. 'Sorry. Didn't mean it. OK?'

'That's all right.'

I walked past her and picked up the second volume of *The Brothers Karamazov*, which was lying on the sofa.

'I'm off then,' I said. 'Bye.'

'Enjoy,' she said.

Now I had an hour to myself. It was the sole condition I had made before taking over responsibility for Vanja during the daytime, that I would have an hour on my own in the afternoon, and even though Linda considered it unfair since she'd never had an hour to herself like that, she agreed. The reason she'd never had an hour, I assumed, was that she hadn't thought of it. And the reason she hadn't thought of it was, I also assumed, that she would rather be with us than alone. But that wasn't how I felt. So for an hour every afternoon I sat in a nearby café reading and smoking. I never went to the same café more than four or five times at a stretch because then they started to treat me like a *stammis*, that is, they greeted me when I arrived and wanted to impress me with their knowledge of my predilections, often with a friendly comment about some topic on everyone's lips. But the whole point for me of living in a big city was that I could be completely alone in it while still surrounded by people on all sides. All with faces I had *never* seen before! The unceasing stream of new faces. For me the very attraction of a big city was immersing myself in that. The Metro swarming with different types and characters. The squares. The pedestrian zones. The cafés. The big malls. Distance, distance, I could never have enough distance. So when a barista began to say hello and smile on catching sight of me and not only brought me a cup of coffee before I asked but also offered me a free croissant, it was time to leave. And it wasn't very hard to find alternatives, we were living in the city centre, and there were hundreds of cafés within a ten-minute radius.

This time I followed Regeringsgatan down towards the centre. It was packed with people. I thought about the attractive woman in the Rhythm Time class as I walked. What had that been all about? I wanted to sleep with her but didn't believe I would get an opportunity, and if I'd had an opportunity I wouldn't have taken it. So why should it be of any importance if I behaved like a woman in front of her?

You can say a lot about my self-image, but it was definitely not shaped in the cool chambers of reason. My intellect may be able to understand it, but it did not have the power to control it. One's self-image not only encompasses the person you are but also the person you want to be, could be or once had been. For the self-image there was no difference between the actual and the hypothetical. It incorporated all ages, all feelings, all drives. When I pushed the buggy all over town and spent my days taking care of my child it was not the case that I was adding something to my life, that it became richer as a result; on the contrary, something was removed from it, part of myself, the bit relating to masculinity. It was not my intellect which made this clear to me, because my intellect knew I was doing this for a good reason, namely that Linda and I would be on an equal footing with regard to our child, but rather my emotions, which filled me with desperation whenever I squeezed myself into a mould that was so small and so constricted that I could no longer move. The question was which parameter should be operative. If equality and fairness were to be the parameters, well, there was nothing to be said about men sinking everywhere into the thralls of softness and intimacy. Nor about the rounds of applause this was met with, for if equality and fairness were the dominant parameters, change was an undoubted improvement and a measure of progress. But these were not the only parameters. Happiness was one; an intense sense of being alive was another. And it may be that women who followed their careers until they were almost in their forties and then at the last moment had a child, which after a few months the father took care of until a place was found in a nursery so that they could both continue their careers, may have been happier than women in previous generations. It was possible that men who stayed at home and looked after their infants for six months may have increased their sense of being alive as a result. And women may actually have desired these men with thin arms, large waistlines, shaven heads and black designer glasses who were just as happy discussing the pros and cons of Baby-bjørn carriers and baby slings as whether it was better to cook one's own baby food or buy ready-made ecological purées. They may have desired them with all their hearts and souls. But even if they didn't, it didn't really matter because equality and fairness were the parameters, they trumped everything else a life and a relationship consisted of. It was a choice, and the choice had been made. For me as well. If I had wanted it otherwise I would have had to back out and tell Linda before she became pregnant: listen, I want children, but I don't want to stay at home looking after them, is that fine with you? Which means, of course, that you're the one who will have to do it. Then she could have said, no, it's not fine with me, or, yes, that's fine and our future could have been planned on that basis. But I didn't, I didn't have sufficient foresight, and consequently I had to go by the rules of the game. In the class and culture we belonged to, that meant adopting the same role, previously called the woman's role. I was bound to it like Odysseus to the mast: if I wanted to free myself I could do that, but not without losing everything. As a result I walked around Stockholm's streets, modern and feminised, with a furious nineteenth-century man inside me. The way I was seen changed, as if at the stroke of a magic wand the

I walked around Stockholm's streets, modern and feminised, with a furious nineteenth-century man inside me

instant I laid my hands on the buggy. I had always eyed the women I walked past, the way men always have, actually a mysterious act because it couldn't lead to anything except a returned gaze, and if I did see a really beautiful woman I might even turn round to watch her, discreetly of course, but nevertheless: why, oh why? What function did all these eyes, all these mouths, all these breasts and waists, legs and bottoms serve? Why was it so important to look at them? When a few seconds, or occasionally minutes, later I had forgotten everything about them? Sometimes I had eye contact, and a rush could go through me if the gaze was held a tiny second longer, because it came from a person in a crowd, I knew nothing about her, where she was from, how she lived, nothing, yet we looked at each other, that was what it was about, and then it was over, she was gone and it was erased from memory for ever. When I came along with a buggy no women looked at me, it was as if I didn't exist. One might think it was because I gave such a clear signal that I was taken, but this was just as evident when I was walking hand in hand with Linda, and that had never prevented anyone from looking my way. My God, wasn't I only getting my just deserts, wasn't I being put in my place for walking around ogling women when there was one at home who had given birth to my child?

No, this was not good.

It certainly was not.

Tonje told me once about a man she had met at a restaurant, it was late, he came over to their table, drunk but harmless, or so they had thought, since he had told them he had come straight from the maternity ward, his partner had given birth to their first baby that day, and now he was on the town celebrating. But then he had started to make advances, he became more and more insistent and in the end suggested they should go back to his ... Tonje was shaken deep into her soul, full of disgust, though also fascination, I suspected, because how was it possible, what was he thinking of?

I couldn't imagine a greater act of betrayal. But wasn't it what I was doing when I sought the eyes of all these women?

My thoughts inevitably went back to Linda sitting at home and washing and dressing Vanja, their eyes, Vanja's inquisitive or happy or sleepy eyes, Linda's beautiful eyes. I had never ever wanted anyone more than her, and now I had not only her but also her child. Why couldn't I be content with that? Why couldn't I stop writing for a year and be a father to Vanja while Linda completed her training? I loved them; they loved me. So why didn't all the rest stop plaguing and harrying me?

I had to apply myself harder. Forget everything around me and just concentrate on Vanja during the day. Give Linda all she needed. Be a good person. For Christ's sake, being a good person, was that beyond me?

© Sam Barker

KARL OVE KNAUSGAARD is a Norwegian writer. His groundbreaking series of six novels entitled *My Struggle* draws heavily on Knausgaard's own life and have become international bestsellers. The first volume, *A Death in the Family*, focuses on the death of his father. *A Man in Love*, from which this Mini is extracted, follows Knausgaard as he moves to Sweden, falls in love and becomes a father himself.

The series caused huge controversy in Norway because of its un-wavering honesty about members of the author's family. As Knausgaard said of the first volume in the *Guardian*: 'The book I had written about myself, which I had seen as an experiment in realistic prose, infinitely dull and uninteresting to others, became a media story for some months in Norway'. The books have also received universal critical acclaim. Jonathan Lethem wrote that Knausgaard is: 'A living hero who landed on greatness by abandoning every typical literary feint, an emperor whose nakedness surpasses royal finery'.

RECOMMENDED BOOKS BY KARL OVE KNAUSGAARD:

A Death in the Family
A Man in Love
Boyhood Island

Where does Fatherhood end up?

Desire
HARUKI MURAKAMI

VINTAGE MINIS

Babies
ANNE ENRIGHT

VINTAGE MINIS

Eating
NIGELLA LAWSON

VINTAGE MINIS

Language
XIAOLU GUO

VINTAGE MINIS

VINTAGE MINIS

The Vintage Minis bring you the world's greatest writers on the experiences that make us human. These stylish, entertaining little books explore the whole spectrum of life – from birth to death, and everything in between. Which means there's something here for everyone, whatever your story.